# CODES

Briane Pagel

GOLDEN FLEECE PRESS

Golden Fleece Press
PO Box 1464,
Centreville, VA 20122
www.goldenfleecepress.com

Special discounts are available on quantity purchases by corporations, associations, and others. For details, contact the publisher at the address above.
U.S. trade bookstores and wholesalers please contact Ingram Content Group at customerservice@ingramcontent.com or by telephone at 800.973.8000(option 3).

PDF ISBN:      978-1-942195-08-5
Mobi ISBN:    978-1-942195-09-2
ePub ISBN:    978-1-942195-11-5
Print ISBN:    978-1-942195-10-8

Printed in the United States of America

First Edition

10 9 8 7 6 5 4 3 2 1

# DEDICATION

To my wife, Joy: all those times I was sort of staring off into space and you asked "What are you thinking about?" and I said *"Nothing,"* I was thinking about the book.  Thanks for putting up with me.

# ACKNOWLEDGMENTS

This book was made possible, and also great, by the following people: my editors and publishers, especially Katherine Ressman, for walking me through the process of turning a pretty good idea into an actually great book, and for making me realize that I start about two-thirds of the sentences I write with the word "and." So much for years of English class.

I also want to thank my good friend Andrew Leon, whose off-hand comment on my blog gave me the idea to write what was supposed to be a short story but just kept on going.

# 1

**You never want to believe you're not you,
but you always knew it didn't you?**

The words were stamped on a poster picturing a vaguely-foreign looking woman staring directly out at the viewer. That was somewhat unusual, in and of itself. Who used prints anymore? It wasn't a screen, wasn't a holo, it was *paper*, a *photograph*, and that, as much as the weird logo and the strangely disconcerting way the woman looked—odd, in a way that couldn't quite be pinned down as odd—was what made the poster stand out.

What also caught Robbie's eye was that the poster hung in the window of a store that had popped up just today. New stores were nothing unusual; this was the kind of minimall in which shops were always opening up today, then disappearing tomorrow: a lunch counter serving real, 'retro' sandwiches, a repair shop for servobots, a souvenir stand;

it seemed like each week there was some new retail outfit doomed to failure for him to walk by on his way to his own job.

*Souvenirs of what?* Robbie wondered when that store had first come (and gone). He rarely noticed the comings-and-goings of the small businesses that failed quickly. Over the time he'd worked at Gravity Sling, probably fifteen of them, each as unappealing and unpromising as the one before, had opened and closed. The only one Robbie had ever gone to was the retro sandwich place. What had it been called? He couldn't remember the name, only why he went there. It wasn't for the actual bread and guaranteed-50%-dairy-cheese on the retro bologna sandwich. It was for the girl, the one with the tight t-shirt and long blond hair, with that slightly blank face that seemed to Robbie as though it was not innocent, or stupid, but uncaring in a way that implied, perhaps, a little bit of sluttiness. He'd gone to the shop every day, so that he could look at that face.

Then the sandwich shop was gone and she was gone and he'd never even learned her name. Life went back to just long tedious days at Gravity Sling—"Send your packages to the orbiters for less! 80% accuracy rating!"—plus longer nights at The Dorms, nights spent hoping he'd find out he had a rich uncle or a rich aunt or perhaps find himself a rich girlfriend—*Ha ha!*—to support him and get him out of this grind.

Rarely was the monotony broken. In the weeks since the sandwich shop had closed, taking away the beauty that had made his sandwiches while he'd watched her hands flattening the bologna and tried to get the nerve to ask her name, only one day stuck out in memory: the day the jerks stopped by.

"Wish I'd been picked for college," Robbie had muttered to himself, that day, saying it as the group, wearing what were obviously Real Suits, came in and handed him a couple of packages to be sent to Orbital 3. *You sure couldn't afford Real Clothes on Gravity Sling wages.* In his mind, he could picture a college campus, what his life would be like if he'd been one of the lucky ones randomly selected to attend. That was his only route in since he didn't come from money and wasn't, so far as he knew, genetically gifted in any way a college would prize; athletically, artistically, or otherwise. His entire life he'd never shown much of a talent for anything, and his aimless drifting through high school had not been the sort of thing that colleges sought out to round out their classes.

"What?" one of the guys had said back to Robbie. He seemed to carry a bit of the outside sunlight with him into the small store, his tan smooth and even, his eyes glinting with superiority. The other guy had the same quality about him—athletic, easy-going in the way of someone who knew they were your boss, almost a glow about him. Like he was *made* better than others. There were three of them, the two guys and a girl. He wondered which of two were a couple, which the odd one out. The girl hung back behind the men at first, and the half-glimpse he got of her nagged at him as he answered:

"Nothing." Robbie turned away and trussed their packages into the heat-resistant baggage. "Did you want to watch?" He looked back towards the group just as the girl bent over to pick something up, and she and the guys caught him inadvertently looking down her shirt. All the way down it.

"No," the taller of the two men had smirked. "But I bet you do."

*Ha ha!*

"You'll get an e-confirm when it launches, and when it's scooped," Robbie muttered. He passed their creds into the slot, waited for the reader to clear them. The girl had stepped away, was looking out the window of the Sling storefront at cars zipping by, heading downtown, uptown, anywhere but the dorms or the crummy part of town where the dorms, and this shop, stood. Robbie glanced over his shoulder at her. Her blonde hair was pulled into a tight businesslike ponytail. She had her arms crossed in a way that suggested she was thinking.

The guys laughed. "Scooped," one of them said, putting a dumb tone into his voice to mock Robbie. He turned to leave, pulling the girl with him. She looked back over her shoulder meeting Robbie's eye. He wished he'd had the nerve to look longer.

She felt *familiar.*

It wasn't until hours later that he managed to finally get the woman out of his thoughts, her image hanging around through all the menial tasks he'd had to work through. Those jerk guys who obviously had jobs where they could afford Real Suits, and probably more than just one—Robbie would bet they had full closets full of different kinds of shirts and pants—they'd faded fairly quickly as his resentment of them slowly boiled away. But the memory of the girl stuck around longer. He found her face floating up in his memory as he fell asleep at night, would realize he was remembering her ponytail, her searching glance at him, and *yes*, her breasts, as he walked from the dorms to his job and back, or wandered around on his days off.

# 2

As he got near work today, Robbie thumbed the tag on his sleeve cuff to alter his changesuit to the outfit Gravity Sling employees were required to wear, an illusion of a polo shirt with the logo of the company emblazoned on it—a stylized Earth sitting in a catapult—in midnight blue, with khaki pants and loafers. Not at all bad looking, even if underneath it was the same heavy, rugged-wear jumpsuit and cloddish boots he wore every day. You could tell the outfit wasn't real without even looking closely, because everything was a little shimmery on a changesuit. But who could afford anything else?

He sighed. He needed something to brighten the day. He found himself thinking of the girl again, hoping she would come back today. That was wishful thinking; nobody needed to sling something twice in a week! It was just as he  realized he'd been hoping the blonde would come back to talk to him— hadn't she caught his eye as she'd left?—that he'd seen the weirdly-exotic looking woman on the poster, with the strange slogan written around her. The sign over the ever-changing shop two doors down from Gravity Sling had altered again. Now it read:

**Find Out Who You Are**

Beneath the sign, which almost seemed to flicker, as if it were old-fashioned neon lighting, were other posters of men, women, families, smiling earnestly at a camera that seemed to be hovering slightly above them, their eyes wide, their smiles not too forced.
*What the?*
The posters each said things like:
> **"I didn't realize who I was until I
> realized who I had been before"**

Or—
> **"We only found each other once
> each of us found himself"**

Or, in the family's case,
> **"Now we know each other!"**

They all seemed so happy. Reading the posters made him slow, almost stumble. He felt uneasy and wanted to look away. Instead, he paused and looked inside the shop. A guy sitting at the counter—his head shaved or completely bald naturally, either way it wasn't a sim—looked up, nodded half-politely at Robbie, met his gaze for perhaps a second too long, then turned back down to looking at something between his elbows, probably a screen.

Robbie looked back up at the sign. "Find Out Who You Are?" he asked softly to himself. The posters kept drawing his eyes back, but he had to get into his job.

He put in a solid five hours of standing around, doing nothing much at all other than waiting for someone to come in and sling something—thirty kilos or less!—into orbit for cheap. Nobody did. He checked the maintenance logs on the sling, made sure the orbital licenses were displayed neatly, and otherwise did busywork, wishing he had a portable screen like the new guy two doors down. Wishing he had anything to occupy his mind, which seemed restless and even more unfocused than usual. He kept glancing towards the outside. He felt jittery.

*Posters.* He kept wondering about that. He knew what they were, of course. Retro posters were sometimes favored by the rich, and of course oldies on the cinema coms had posters in them, so he knew, vaguely, that people used to use paper to advertise things, but it seemed so archaic to him, worse even than when politicians used old-fashioned cars for campaigns. These posters didn't seem designed to appeal to nostalgia, or collectors. They were unsettling. Just looking at them had made him uneasy, the way a dark alley or a group of strangers could cause one to want to shy away. The weird slogans, the strange way the people in the posters looked—all of them seeming, somehow, *not quite*...he couldn't put his finger on it. Not quite *right.*

When he got done with work, after what seemed ages, the new shop appeared closed. Robbie walked up to the front window and peered inside, the glare from streetlights helping him see, but there was not much to look at. A countertop. A wall behind it. He saw for the first time a poster on the wall behind where the bald clerk had sat. This one showed a man, stern and somewhat frowning, a contrast to the happy people in the photos in the window. The man had close-cropped hair, little more than sparse stubble. His eyes appeared too green. He stared down the bridge of his nose and his mouth was serious. Written underneath the man, in block letters: **NOW, YOU KNOW.**

Robbie stared at that poster, and some of the others. The gloom of night made them hard to see. After a few minutes, he tore himself away and made his way home, feeling a bit dizzy.

He laid awake for a long time, his screen turned to music, random shapes swirling in time to the soft beats. Finally about midnight he got up and did a search for "Find Out Who You Are." The first result was a link to what seemed to be the company's site and he clicked on it. Almost instantly the screen started filling with popped-windows of dozens of people talking:

"I always felt like maybe it was weird—"

"I'd never heard of the place—"

"—husband told me that wasn't like me..."

"I was someone else..."

"—you know, wasn't satisfied with what I was doing..."

"—felt things were supposed to be different..."

"—never thought I'd find out I wasn't—"

More and more, each talking over the other, saying strange-sounding things. He watched them as the screen filled, and once it was full, they began to one by one dim and disappear until only the central one remained. It was the stern man from the poster in the shop, his eyes gazing straight out of the middle of the screen. The face seemed to come to a point, almost – the man's brows furrowed down over eyes that were so thinly opened they at first appeared closed, a straight nose leading one's gaze directly to the mouth, a pencil-thin frown. From there, though, those eyes pulled the viewer back up: they didn't appear sleepy at all: from underneath the heavy lids, even the whites of the eyes appeared to smolder with some sort of fervor.

*Angry?* Robbie thought. He looked at the eyes again. *Alive.* The word popped into his head. *Alive like fire.*

The man said, "Welcome To Find Out Who You Are. I am Koss Ernst. Find Out Who You Are can tell you exactly Who. You. Are." As he said those words, they appeared on the screen, surrounding his head in capital letters and punctuation.

"This isn't some sort of personality test. This isn't some kind of cult, or job-training site. Do not get the wrong idea. Find Out Who You Are does not dabble in psychiatry, or psychology, or horoscopes and wish-fulfillment."

There was a pause. The man stared out at Robbie, meaningfully.

"Find Out Who You Are will do just that. It will discover who is the real you. We use technology that I devised on my own, technology that has helped make all of these people not just happy—" Here the people's bubbles reopened and they began smiling, a 3-d set of heads and shoulders grinning and talking in murmurs. "But made them certain of their identity—not of their likes or dislikes or need for companionship or which job they might like better, but their *identity*. And they, and the other clients I have, are the only people who actually have that knowledge about themselves. The only people who Know. Who. They. Are."

Again as Koss Ernst said those words, they appeared on the screen, this time reading:

**Know. Who. You. Are.**

"That's... I know who I am," Robbie said.

**Do**

**You**

**?**

—flashed on the screen. Robbie slid back on his chair, just a bit.

"Nice trick," he said. Probably, the guy had guessed that many people, like him, would respond with a statement enough like the one Robbie had used, and had programmed the site to flash that in order to make it seem as though someone was listening to him. "Nicely done," he added. He reached up and pressed a button to turn the screen off entirely when

"RAP-RAP-RAP-RAP-POUND-RAP-RAP-RAP-POUND"

Robbie nearly jumped out of his skin as a sound—like someone trying very hard to knock through his door with just knuckles—echoed around him off the bare walls and tiled floor.

He stood up and looked at the front door of his Cubicle.

"Who is it?" he said quietly.

There was no answer.

He walked hesitantly towards the door and put his ear against it, listening, holding his breath. He felt his pulse in his neck, his forehead, his fingertips, and when he realized that, he quickly pulled his hands away from the door lest the person on the other side somehow be able to detect the thud of blood in his veins and arteries.

"Who is it?" he said again, more loudly.

Still no answer. The Dorms' cubicles didn't have view-screens or anything like that on their doors. He'd never regretted that much, before; usually the door was left open anyway when he was just hanging out, was only locked when he went to bed. Or when he had a girl up here, which was rare, as he could never afford one and Free Girls mostly didn't date Dormers.

He slowly opened the door, and saw the guy from the weird store, the counter guy, standing there, holding a screen in his hand, not looking at Robbie. He was instead staring down the hallway, which faded away into a bland, dimly-lit muted brown of carpet and plastic panel walls, his eyes wide, his mouth open as though he was gasping for air.

"What the..." Robbie said, and looked in the direction the man was looking, but saw nothing.

The man from the store collapsed in a heap at his feet with a firm *thud*, his changesuit shimmering back from the outfit he wore to a plain gray jumpsuit as the bioenergy that powered it faded because the man was dying. Or was already dead. The screen dropped from the man's hand and Robbie saw a little blood trickle from the man's nose. He bent down, put his fingers to the man's neck, feeling for a pulse and knowing he wouldn't get one.

"You killed him!" a woman yelled out from his left, then started screaming.

Robbie looked up to see the blonde woman from a few days before standing there in the hallway, pointing at him and the dead man and screaming even more loudly.

"No," he said. "No, no no..."

*NO NO NO NO*, echoed in his head.

But she wasn't listening. She kept screaming. Doors were opening all around the hallway, guys coming out with sleepy eyes and bed hair and the occasional girl behind them, all staring at him, at the body, at the blonde. His neighbor, Tomas, stepped over.

"Elsie? What's wrong?"

"You know her?" Robbie asked, standing up and looking at Tomas.

"Know her? Robbie, what?"

"Tomas! Oh, Tomas!" Elsie sobbed, rushing to him and throwing her arms around him. "Oh, my god, Tomas, call Security, I saw it all! This guy was bringing us the screen I ordered Robbie for our anniversary"

*What?*

"And Robbie just KILLED HIM!"

Tomas spun around, staring at Robbie.

"Jesus, Robbie,"

*Jesus H. Christ is more like it... what the...?*

There were already sirens. Robbie did the only thing he could think of: he backed into his apartment, pushing the door closed as Tomas tried to grab him, saying "Robbie Robbie, what's going on?"

Elsie stared at him, her head still on Tomas' shoulder, as he shoved the door closed tightly. He saw that and also saw the dead man's hand push the screen through the crack of the door before it latched shut, a sight that didn't register until after he'd lock-sealed the door, heart pounding worse than ever.

He picked up the tablet, but he still couldn't think of anything to do other than stand there, dumbly, mouth open, staring at the door. Something in his spinal column—maybe that fabled reaction center from the times when humans were lizard-like and better able to react to danger without all the thinking—made him stumble backwards and sit on his bed.

In front of him, on his big wall screen, the words **Do You?** were still front and center on the cloud display and the people talking in bubble windows began to get louder and louder again. In the center of it all was Koss

Ernst, staring at him mutely, eyebrows narrowed, chin held a little too high, nose a severe stabbing wedge pointed right at him.

His handheld screen rang. He looked down, touched it to answer.

"Yes?"

"Security! Permission to enter?" The screen showed a battle-masked face looming. Before he could speak another line on the screen rang. He stared into the visor-covered face staring up at him from the handheld unit as he quickly touched the screen to answer the second line.

"Robbie!" a voice said.

The voice was Koss Ernst's voice, the same voice Robbie had heard only moments before on the wall-screen.

Robbie looked over at the second half of the screen.

"Put me on mute! Or hang up!'

"Permission to enter is not needed!" the security officer yelled through his half of the small unit. "If you do not admit us we will simply enter."

"Hang up!" Koss Ernst said.

Robbie froze in confusion. But Koss said it again—*"Hang up!"*—and his voice was so commanding that Robbie obeyed, jabbing a thumb on the left half of the screen. Immediately, a pound came at the door, and the muffled voice of the security officer demanded the door be opened. He must really have been calling from outside in the hall, Robbie realized, but Koss Ernst was talking already.

"Take this screen with you and jump out the window," he said.

*Jump?* Robbie's face must have showed his confusion.

"Do it," Koss Ernst continued. "Do you know how long we have been looking for you? We need you to get back to us."

The door opened up. Two men from Security rushed in and grabbed Robbie. One took the screen away from him as the other slapped a collar around his neck, locking it quickly.

"Robbie, you are under arrest for the murder of Jensen. You will accompany us to the station where you are required to answer our questions. Resistance of any of these directives may result in stunning. Do you have a heart condition?"

Robbie shook his head no.

They took him roughly by the arms and began leading him out of his apartment and into the hallway, where he no longer saw Tomas, or the blonde girl, or the dead man. The hall was empty.

$$3$$

"How long do you think he'll sleep?"

"How long has it been now?" A woman's voice.

"Two hours." That was a different person. *So there were at least three...*

"Any minute now." The same woman.

"Better for him if he doesn't wake up." The second man again.

"It doesn't need to be like that." That was the first man.

"It always ends up like that." Woman again.

"This one might be different." A man's voice, again. Through the clearing haze in his head, Robbie tried to figure out where the three were standing around him. Something in him told him to do this, told him he did not want to open his eyes or let them know he was awake, even though they could probably tell.

The first man was closest to him, he decided.

"They never are." The second man had moved in, from wherever he'd been a moment ago.

"Took you long enough to figure out," the woman lectured.

"Took them just as long." First man. Defensive.

"Not quite 'just as long.' They'd practically set up shop already." The woman was in charge. He realized he knew her voice.

"*Practically.* But we were already watching him, before that," the second man said. He was defensive now, too.

"You were *watching* him before that," the woman replied. Her voice was very quiet, and very near Robbie's face.

"Yeah. *Watching.* And I didn't see *you* figuring him out that day. And how were we supposed to know he was one if *you* didn't figure it—" the first man asked before he was interrupted by the second.

"Yeah. How come you *didn't* recognize—"

"Fuck you," the woman interrupted.

"I only do Free Girls," the second man said. But his voice was too quiet to make it an effective insult, and then silence drew over them all.

*She is definitely in charge* Robbie thought and wondered at the part of him that was somehow just cataloging what was going on around him.

"He's waking up," the woman said.

Robbie couldn't hide it anymore. He opened his eyes as two men stepped out into the hall. Before he could recognize them, they were out the door.

He sat in a small bed with metal rails on either side, but the rails were down. He was still groggy, and was disoriented by his surroundings, all the more so because he didn't remember falling asleep. He didn't remember anything after the scene in the apartment.

He looked around the room, bewildered, saw the bed he was on, a table and chair, and nothing else. The walls were beige, empty. The kind of walls that in a hospital would have been meant to be calming, but here they looked somehow eerily scientific and made him uneasy. His head felt flickery, like he'd just left off looking at a strobe light. He supposed he must be somewhere inside Security, or a Security Annex, at least, and wondered if he'd fainted.

*Do you have a heart condition?*

He hadn't thought he did.

As he looked from the doorway the men had gone out to the walls on his left and back to his right, his mind taking all this in and trying to sort it out, the knowledge that the woman must still be in the room floated up through his mind. He turned all the way to his right, saw her standing up behind his shoulder, at the head of the bed, almost behind him.

It was the blonde from the hall, from the shop with the two jerks. He stared at her, trying simultaneously to wrap his head around where he was and who she was. His mind reassembled the scene in the hall where she'd not only claimed she'd known him and Tomas but had accused him—*falsely! Right? He hadn't done anything, had he?*—of murder. He'd recognized her then from the day at the store, and now realized that her visit to Gravity Sling must not have been an accident. *How come you didn't recognize him?* one of the men had asked.

"Hello?" she asked, the inflection in her voice making it clear she wasn't sure he was ready to talk yet.

Robbie sat there a second, then: "Do I have to answer your questions?" A pause. "Legally, I mean?" *Where did that come from* he wondered? Underneath the roiling of his surface thoughts he could almost sense a sort of calm, like there was another person, a friend, there with him telling him to just relax.

"Of course you do." She held up her arm, showed him the badge tattooed there. He hadn't noticed it that day when she'd come into the store with the two guys. Of course, that meant nothing. Electrically-activated skin inks had been around for generations, and if she'd been told not to show her badge it wouldn't have been visible. Plus he hadn't had much time that day to look at her. And he hadn't exactly been looking at her forearm. "But let's first see if you're feeling better."

"Feeling better?"

"Quite a scare you gave those... cops," she said. "Stopping breathing?"

"I..." Robbie closed his mouth. *Cops?* They were Security. Nobody ever saw cops anymore. Robbie couldn't even have said where a police station was.

While he wondered why she'd pretended the men who'd taken him in were police, the woman pulled the chair from the table, sat down across from him. Her hands were folded together on her skirt. The skirt looked like it was Real, not a changesuit.

"I suppose it was just the stress," she said.

*Sure, yes, all right.* "Sure," he said aloud.

"When the man attacked you?"

Robbie eyed her.

"The man attacked you, right?"

"You... he... I know you from..." *from the sandwich shop.* The thought leapt into his brain. He stared at her more intently. *That can't be right, can it?*

He was feeling confused and assumed that was secondary to having been stunned by the collar. Although she seemed to be saying that hadn't happened?

The blonde was holding up her arm again, the badge glowing—recording. "I am sure," she said, "that the man attacked you, Robbie. I was there, as you know, to ask you questions about contacts you'd had with someone we want to talk to when that man came out of the elevator. He compared you to a picture he had on his screen, and he attacked you. You had to stun him, I believe that, and I was there to see the whole thing."

*Then you know that's not...* Robbie kept his mouth closed. She continued, moving in towards him. "I am sure that is what—" she leaned a little closer, still, so close that Robbie could see individual strands of blonde hair, two, three, falling over her eyes. He had to restrain himself from leaning forward and gently brushing them out of her way.

*Whoa...*

"—could easily be proven to be true, provided that we know what the man said to you just before you stunned him with your own handheld."

Robbie looked straight at her eyes, which were not in any way matching the sincere-seeming smile on her face. The eyes had no humor in them. The eyes told him he should very carefully listen to her and not be distracted by the smile. The eyes were beautifully frightening. As he looked at them he wanted them to soften, and somehow knew that they could. Finally, because her eyes remained cold and grim, he looked away from them to her smile, which also looked familiar. More than it should from that brief day in the store.

"Then, with that proven, this all becomes simply a quick case of self-defense and you are heading back home, although given that your cubicle is a crime scene we would probably have to arrange for housing for you Uptown."

*Uptown?*

"Temporarily, of course, but you know how those things sometimes might take years to be untemporaried."

Robbie looked down at his hands, then up at her again. She lifted her arm again, showed him the glowing badge there.

*God, my head is spinning.*

Maybe he had a concussion or something. Robbie was about to say so, to ask for some aspirin or a painswab, when another thought came to him,

*It's not a headache.* That felt true, even if he didn't know why he'd thought it.

"I need some time to think," he said.

She leaned back, then, and stared at him coolly.

"No." her voice was flat. "Your time expired when I finished my last sentence." She stood up, pushed the chair to the side. The door opened again, and the two men came back in.

With a start, Robbie realized they were the college-guys, the guys who had come into the store that day and caught him looking at the woman. He stared from them back to the blonde. She'd turned away as the men entered, and when he saw her profile he suddenly realized: she was not only the woman from the hall and the visit with these two jerks but was also, after all, the sandwich shop girl, too.

*What the...*

"Come with us, Robbie," one of the guys said, and he had the same amount of snark in his voice that he'd had that other day.

*So that hadn't been an act.*

# 4

"Here's the thing," the blonde said. "There is a rumor going around, perhaps one you've heard, or seen on posters? Perhaps someone brushed against you in the hallway and whispered something. Or possibly a girl, having gotten her money and being ready to leave, turned around and said something, something like—"

*Nobody is who they think they are.*

"Nobody is who they think they are?" she finished.

*The pretty girl on the tram had said that.*

Sights flashed through his head: He was holding onto the handle of the tram. Amidst tall buildings. Not just tall buildings—*skyscrapers.* He was never around skyscrapers. They flew past outside the elevated tracks. A girl had been looking at him. Robbie had been wearing a suit. Two men had approached him. A man with a shaved head.

He jerked his body and arched his back. He realized, as the blonde's words sunk in and the vision of the elevated train receded, that he was a captive. He was hanging vertically, hands above his head, lights in his eyes, feet strapped to the floor, stomach aching from whatever they'd pumped into his throat. The blonde had paused. The room was silent and smelled like cleanser. He wondered what he was supposed to say.

"Or maybe," one of the college-guys said, "Maybe a store opened up right next to you, and they said you could find out who you are and maybe they'd even do it on your lunch break."

Robbie couldn't turn his head to look at the guy: the collar was back on. He felt like he was going to vomit, and tried to hold it back. He wouldn't be able to look down, or away from the girl, and didn't want to throw up all over her. Plus, he wasn't sure he wouldn't choke on it, the way they had him strung up. He tried to close his throat. The posters in the darkened window of the store flashed through his mind, and he saw the guy with the screen nod at him again.

"And maybe" the college guy continued, "You went in there, talked to him? Searched for his business on your screen? Got a phone call from the owner of the business?"

The man's face was right in front of his, and Robbie burped, not minding doing that to *this* guy. *Make fun of me?* He thought. "I'm gonna barf," he said, and the man pulled back. Robbie wanted to smile but couldn't.

*Victories are sometimes small!*

"Did you talk to him, Robbie?" The woman said again.

His stomach wrenched and tumbled, and he did throw up. She nimbly stepped away and the floor briefly skizzed while cleanersonics scrubbed the trio's feet. None of them reacted in any overt way otherwise. Interrogation rooms are used to people getting sick. So are interrogators.

"Did you talk to any of them, Robbie?" the college guy asked.

The other college guy had been going over Robbie's skin—Robbie was naked, and cold, and now had vomit on him—with a scanner of some sort, inch by inch by inch.

"He's clean," the other guy now said. "They haven't."

*Haven't what?*

"OK," the girl said. She turned abruptly and walked out, the college guys behind her, leaving Robbie alone in the room. It smelled faintly now of his own puke mixed with whatever they'd shoved into the tube they'd pushed into his throat before they'd begun questioning him.

After a few minutes, the motion-activated lights went off. Robbie hung there, in the dark, his arms slowly going numb from a lack of circulation, neck stiff from holding his head up, nostrils and mouth stinging from the residue of the bile that had just passed through them. His mind spun in his head, dizzying. He tried to sort through images of the three questioners coming into the GravitySling, of the man with the screen in the shop next door, but kept having flashes of the same man falling to the ground outside his door, and that same man pressing up to him on the tram, next to the other girl who'd just spoken to him. They'd pressed something to his head... he shook his head, but it was not enough to clear things up, or to turn the lights back on.

# 5

*"Everybody is someone else.*
*that's how they get you...*
*and how they keep you."*
**FIND OUT WHO YOU ARE**

//Robbie you are not dreaming.//
"Who?"
*Who?*
//This is all real.//
"Who?"
*What the...?*
//You are a Code. Listen to me carefully and remember that, if you remember nothing else: **You are a Code**.//
"I... am a Code."
*Oh God, I'm going to throw up again.*
//We are all, in the end, Codes but some of us more than others.//
*Am I supposed to repeat that?*

//This is going to be hard to understand.//

"Who is talking?"

//Nobody is talking. This is in your head.//

"I'm dreaming, then. Dreaming. Or hallucinating."

"He's awake, and saying something." Robbie faintly heard the college guy, the leader, saying somewhere off in the distance.

"Get in there!" The sandwich shop girl... no, not her. The girl with the jerk guys. Or was it?

//You are not dreaming. This is not a dream. They're coming to get you, right now. I should have told you not to talk. We have little time, so listen carefully: you are a Code, and you need to...//

"Hold him!" College Guy 2 snarling, hands on Robbie's face.

"ARRGGHGGGH!" Robbie cried out in anguish. He couldn't help howling as a shock jolted from the collar through his shoulders and down into his chest.

"Who are you talking to?" It *was* sandwich shop girl. It was her voice. He kept his eyes shut. Was it her?

//Tell them nobody.//

"Nobody! I'm talking to—ARGHGGHGHA GOHGODARGGGAHH! Robbie felt like they were pulling his spine out through his skin. Something was digging into him, into his nerves. A wrenching, twisting pull that spread from the middle of his back out through his arms and up into his head. He realized they'd stuck something *into* him. Into his *neck*. The pulling was an illusion: something was pushing into him. He felt cold seeping out from the base of his skull, making every nerve it touched feel as though it was tightening. And inside his head his brain started feeling crystalline, brittle, as though each cell in it had been converted to a tiny shard of glass and then started cracking.

*I hope I die.*

"WHO are you talking to?"

//Don't answer.//

"I don't know." The hands were pulling at his head, which was starting to feel jelly-like inside. He couldn't feel his fingers. It suddenly struck him that they were not doing anything to his *nerves.*

//They are draining your *mind.*//

"Tell us." She was somehow both girls at the same time. *Why was her voice so familiar?* Robbie struggled to think straight.

"I *don't* know!" he screamed out.

With a burst of energy his mind lit up inside and he could almost *see* it. It felt like it was glowing, a volcanic eruption of thought. Images and sounds and smells broke free and flooded his senses even as his legs went numb. His heart stopped, for just a second.

//They are close.//

"ARGHGHGIidon'tknowidon'tknowidon'tk nowAAAIIIIIGGGH." He tried to make them understand something he himself could not understand.

*He was starting first grade holding dad's hand*

//Too close. I am sorry, Robbie.//

*He was entering a boardroom, to a brief round of nods welcoming him to the upper echelon*

//Go to sleep now,// the voice inside told him.

//TTTCCACAGAAGGAT//

"We've lost him," he heard. He wanted to ask which blonde she was, the sandwich shop worker or the mean one with the guys, or was she both?

But he had no time. His consciousness, each of them, faded.

# 6

**"Wanted for Espionage:
Koss Ernst.
Reward.
Contact Security if seen."**

"Well, can we reverse engineer him? Figure out if he really is one?" said the blonde woman's supervisor, sitting at his desk and staring at his operatives. "And, if so, what is it this one's supposed to do?"

The broad expanse of desk between them was entirely bare but for two screens, each of which flickered numerous windows of information that the supervisor occasionally glanced at during these talks. But for now he just met their gazes, waited for each of them to look away. First one of the men, then the other, broke off and glanced down at the carpet, or over at the wall where there were prints, actual *paintings*, hanging. The supervisor favored still lifes. A wall of fruits in bowls, and glasses slightly in shadow, and one picture that showed various birds hanging from a ledge in a kitchen waiting to be plucked and cooked, sat mutely. Put there not just to emphasize that the supervisor could buy such things, but also to draw the eyes of those who sat across the desk from him.

The blonde refused to look away. She had never once looked at the stupid pictures. She stared straight at the supervisor. "We are certain he is one," she said slowly. "We've been tracking him for a while now, and—"

"You're sure. Why, because he lives in the dorms and is a loser?" her supervisor interrupted. His eyes rose to the large screen, behind the operatives, on the wall across from him, showing stock prices sliding along on various lines, red for bad, yellow for neutral, green for good. He watched for the company's stock as he talked at them. Was it up? Down? Neutral? "That's not proof."

The blonde kept looking at him until he pulled his eyes back down to her before she spoke. She tried not to smile at the victory. "Because—and I know what I'm doing— he was contacted directly by Koss," she told him. He looked only at her face. She was impressed despite herself: most men never looked away from her tits. Her supervisor never looked at them. His determination not to be distracted by them mirrored her resolve not to look at his stupid paintings of vegetables and other inanimate objects. She got the joke: *still life. Inanimate.* She didn't think much of it, wanted to tell him *they're not inanimate, moron. Created people are not* things. But she knew she was too defensive around him already and wouldn't give him the satisfaction.

"So, what, you're saying is that Koss has a way of tracking them?"

"We think so. We're already trying to reverse-engineer this one. We obtained genetic material directly from his intestinal lining, and we've found the three markers that show it was Koss. What we're trying to do is figure out what this version is supposed to do."

The supervisor didn't remark on how they'd been too slow to get the brain scan done. The three of them had only been outside in the hall for two minutes, waiting for the cart, when they'd heard the talking. Without discussing it, none of them had volunteered that information at all, that they'd stepped outside the room. Who could've known the captive could do a thing like that, anyway?

"How long until we know?" he asked her. He put his hands on the desk now, and she wondered if that was to help him keep looking directly at her when he so clearly wanted to look away. How many times a day did he play this little power game? Did he do it with everyone? Or just her and her people?

"We may not, at all." There were no reports in the system yet about the way the man's brain had just...*shut down.*

"So we just hold him?"

"Well, unless you want to kill him."

She could tell the supervisor hadn't made up his mind about that, yet, and wondered why that was. It couldn't be that killing Robbie would be trouble. It wouldn't be, in any sense, as it wasn't illegal and couldn't be traced.

Even if the man had moral qualms about killing—and she knew he didn't—Robbie was no more human to him than the game he'd been playing earlier on his handheld screen, or one of his stupid paintings. She knew from dealing with him this long that he felt more empathy for the company stock than he did for one of the Codes. She tried not to take that the wrong way, but couldn't really help it. Still, obviously there was no sentimentality causing him to hesitate about whether or not to destroy the Robbie.

"He could still be useful to us, right?" the man asked, now.

"Potentially."

"We could get his code into the mainframe and then destroy this one. With the code safe, we could create new ones if we need to, and still figure out why this one seems so important to them."

"I wouldn't recommend copying his code yet." Neither of her men looked at her as she said that. *Good.* They knew enough not to even react, so that there was no suggestion made to the supervisor they *couldn't* get it. She went on: "Put it in the database—assuming it's not there already—put this Robbie's code in a database, anywhere, even a separate drive, and you make it copyable and creatable." The blonde tried not to visibly hold her breath. Would he recognize her ploy? If the code was useful, if it could be obtained and was any good, it would be useful only to those who understood it, and only those who had access to it could understand it. The upper execs would look past almost anything that held you back from promotion, if you came up with something valuable enough. She didn't know if they'd *get* the code from the Robbie, but she was damned if she was going to go to all this trouble and then just pass it on...

"So we keep him alive."

"For now," the blonde agreed, and she stood up. The supervisor hadn't dismissed her but she risked the slight insubordination anyway. She felt him watching as he left, but on the big screen the company stock scrolled by again, and she knew he would be diverted by that, and that in moments he would be back to reviewing the new pitch they were going to make to the team owners next week, and would have largely let the matter of the Robbie fade from his mind as he focused on that.

# 7



The blonde stepped through the door into the lab and looked around. She saw only two techs, only one of whom was working on the Robbie. She watched him for a moment, then looked over at the glowing outlines of chromosomes on the terminals that lined the shelves. Scrolling screen after screen of C and G and A and T and, of course, H, that additional, synthetic nucleotide, each in varying combinations, whirled over and over on several of the monitors. After trying to make sense of them, she asked, "Any progress?"

The tech shrugged.

"This one's way different than anything I've ever seen. We maybe need someone more experienced in here."

"Didn't you find *anything* yet?"

"Well..." The tech touched an area of a screen near his left arm. The image froze with TGGGTT glowing over and over on it. "Stuff like this seems... ominous."

"Ominous?"

"Yeah. Threatening. Weird and threatening. Hard to know what to make of it." The tech was touching other areas of the screen, and first the G and then the T would light up. He pushed them around, showed her how different configurations appeared in various types of Codes they'd already created, talking about how putting a few Gs in a row like that, embedding them here and *here*, for example, would heighten aggression, while the *T* usually meant adaptability but nobody ever paired it up that way, not two Ts in a row, even with the extra spaces built onto the DNA sequence in Codes. "It's not like he's an assassin or something..." the tech trailed off.

The blonde couldn't take her eyes off the screens now, showing the Robbie broken down into his DNA sequences "...but?" she asked, filling in the void left by the tech's silence.

"But he is dangerous." The tech sat back down. "Or so it would seem. At least there's the potential for it in that DNA. So dangerous, probably, it would help to know what he was *doing.* At least the last few days, if not longer."

The blonde looked around the lab. She agreed, but didn't feel like telling the tech that they hadn't been able to break into the Robbie's mind yet. Instead she tapped one of the screens. "You haven't copied any of this stuff anywhere, have you?" she asked.

"No."

"And all you've done is check the DNA and RNA sequences so far, right? I don't want anyone trying to do a brain scan on him."

The tech assured her nobody had even gone into the room where the Robbie still sat, unconscious. *And with his mind locked up like a vault*, the blonde thought. She looked over at the other set of test tubes and readings, the ones from the dead man outside Robbie's door. Time to change the subject before the tech wondered *why* they weren't following protocol and scanning the Robbie now, the way they always did. "What about this one?" She tried to remember what his corpse had looked like, laying in the hallway. She remembered track-star muscles, the bald head and creamy-brown skin that reminded her of the color of nougat. As she bent and looked into a beaker where some of the man's spinal fluid was being destructively distilled, she had a vision of his hands. They had seemed gentle. *Pianist hands*, she thought, and wondered when she had ever seen a piano in real life.

The tech looked at her and shrugged again. "On the one hand, it would seem he's a fairly typical Code. Surface-wise there's nothing remarkable about him so far as I can tell—"

She interrupted him. "What was it that killed him? A Ping?" That would've taken the man out, she knew. The tiny projectiles could destroy internal organs while leaving almost no marks outside the skin. That was what they were designed for. Little BB-sized pellets shot from guns with the power of a bazooka, the surface coated in a nanometer of friction-reducing coating, so that it would enter the skin quickly and then stay inside the body, ricocheting over and over until it had turned everything inside the area it hit into paste.

"We don't know," said the other tech.

"You don't know?"

"Nope. No cause of death we can discern. That's what I was starting to tell you." The tech got up again, walked over to the various slides and samples, slid one into a reader and a screen above it lit up.

The blonde remembered the Code bleeding, as if he'd been shot. Stagecraft? She looked at the screen as the tech fiddled with it, brought it into a closer focus. "What about his memories?" she asked. The slide below was being scanned by several hair-thin green laser lines, but the readout from them was showing nothing, just the dashes used to indicate empty storage space. Before the tech could answer, she realized what she was looking at. "He doesn't have any memories?" She asked it mostly to herself. Leaning across the man, she tapped a few keys, watched the lasers scan again, watched the readout show no results again. "He doesn't have any," she echoed herself more faintly this time. Her facial expression grew intense but then froze in a blank mask.

The blonde thought about the neck wound she'd seen, and then pictured the Code shoving the screen into the Robbie's door with its too-delicate hands. Her mind worked furiously. The man had not been dead when he'd hit the floor. That much was clear. But he'd been dead when Security picked him up. And now his body held *no* memories at all. A dead man with no memories could only mean one of two things: either all electrical activity in the brain had ceased long enough prior to the scan to degrade the cells so badly the lasers were unable to detect the code, or the brain had been wiped clean prior to the scan.

The man had been dead less than two minutes when his brain had been sliced open. She knew full well that wasn't enough time for the memories implanted in there during the cloning process to have been destroyed by ordinary organic decay. Almost *none* of the storage should have been harmed. The brain itself was intact.

Someone had wiped this man's mind.

But she had seen the man, seen him standing there in the hall, seen him doing things: even if the man's mind had been wiped clean prior to that, there should be a memory of those last few moments. She had been standing next to him! Even if they'd erased his mind before whoever he was came up to the Robbie's door, there should be a memory of the walk up the stairs, knocking on the door, shoving the screen forward. Nobody had wiped those last few moments, she was sure.

A thought occurred to her. "Basic bios?" she asked softly.

"Nothing," the tech said. His voice sounded as baffled as she felt. The man's brain had no record, even, of making his heart beat, of making his lungs breathe, of anything. His mind was like a blank computer chip, waiting for something, anything, to be recorded on it.

Impossible.

"A fairly typical Code," The blonde said, with enough sarcasm to make the tech wince a bit. He started to say something but she interrupted. "Where's the body?"

"Melted."

"And the codes?"

"Secured," the tech said.

"I'll be the judge of that. Where?"

The tech held up a small cube, less than 1 cm on each side. The blonde took it. "When did you load it?"

"About an hour ago."

"Where's the cube been since then?"

"In my pocket."

"Okay." The blonde took the cube, put it in her own pocket. She wondered whether she should kill the tech. Then she'd have to take out the other one, too, especially since she didn't know how much he'd overheard. As she pondered it she tried to picture how she'd cover *that* up, decided it was too much trouble for now. There was no reason to think the tech would report any time soon.

She started giving orders. "Don't store any of the Robbie's information, at all. Not even on cubes. I'm going to try to talk to him one more time. If he won't tell me anything, we'll scan him and melt him."

"Fine."

The blonde walked outside the room, where the two operatives were waiting. She frowned at them. "This time," she said, "You wait outside for a bit longer." She walked ahead of them, wishing she could push her sleeves down over her tattoo without them noticing. They reached the interrogation room, and she walked inside alone, the lights flickering on as she did so.

The Robbie hung before her, naked and reeking of vomit and head lolling to the side. She saw it fight through a half-unconscious near-sleep state as the lights woke him up. The door shut behind her and before anyone said anything, she pushed her sleeves down and held her hand over the tattoo under her sleeve. It was better than nothing. She didn't *think* her supervisor could tap into it without her knowing about the intrusion, if not exactly consenting to it. But she also knew there might be lots of things they had put into her that she could not control, and might not ever even be aware of.

"Robbie," she said, in her softest voice. The smell gagged her a bit, but she forced herself to stand closer to the Code.

It goggled at her, eyes trying to focus. She saw the hands dangling limply, fingers a bit blue at the tips.

"Would you like to get out of that? Sit for a bit?"

It nodded, weakly.

"Then tell me, Robbie: are you who you think you are?"

The eyes stared at her. They were focused, almost, but still a bit glassy seeming. She couldn't tell if it this was an act. She bit her lip, hiding her anger. "Robbie: are you who you think you are?"

It closed the eyes again. "Can't feel my fingers," the mouth mumbled.

"I'll let you sit down as soon as you answer my question. Are you who you think you are?"

The eyes stayed closed. She snapped her fingers under its nose, sharply, and as she did so, the eyes opened, wide, and she saw the whites all around the pupils. It snarled at her and bit her fingers, grabbing them with its teeth, pulling the head back sharply. She felt tearing, ripping, bleeding, and there was a horrible feeling in her hand as it nearly ripped her index finger off.

She yelled and the two operatives came charging through the door, one with a stun gun that he hit the Robbie with in the neck— she felt the jolt in her own arm, all the way to the elbow—and the other pushing a forearm into its stomach. The Robbie's body was held taut in the restraints, so the blow caused it's breath to whoosh out, and it let go of her finger even as the muscles in its body clenched tighter from the stun charge. The blonde fell back, pressing her hand into her armpit. She felt as much as saw the crackle of electricity rippling over and over the body from the stunner.

"Enough!" she yelled. The man with the stun gun stopped, and she ordered a medic and a brain scan team immediately.

"You've reached the end of the road, Robbie," she said. In moments someone would be here to reattach her finger, and to find out what the fuck this Code knew.

> **To: Home://xt.Alex.Keith//URG.**
>
> **{picture attached}** Alex, this was my sister. MY SISTER.
>
> **AK:** Koss, what is your point?
>
> **KE:** She died two years ago.
>
> **AK:** I'm very sorry, but I don't see why you are telling me.
>
> **KE:** Yesterday, I saw her working in tech.
>
> **EMP ACCT: TERMINATED**
>
> **EMP STATUS: DETAIN**

Koss Ernst read through the exchange again, then folded the paper up and tucked it back into his pants pocket. The paper had grown weak along the seams of the folds, it had been opened and closed so many times. He sat back down on the couch, listening to the bustle in the other room, the kitchen they'd converted into a lab. He didn't want to be right there when they woke her up.

*"You* have *to promise to keep waking me up,"* she'd told him, once.

He pictured telling her how it had felt to watch her die, watch the monitor showing her heartbeat slowing to a straight line, her hands stop fluttering. He imagined telling her what it had felt like to see her sitting in the Greenhouse, leaning over one of the tubes that he'd never understood the purpose of, let alone what it had felt like when she'd suddenly showed up at the small apartment he'd been hiding out in down in one of the crummier areas of the city, telling him that she needed him, needed his genius, needed him to carry on what he'd started at the company.

But all that had fallen away and he'd hugged her and started crying and then she'd made him promise.

*"Promise,"* she'd said again.

He'd promised, and he'd tried to make it believable, but a part of him couldn't stand seeing her go out over and over into a world where she could keep dying and then be remade again sometimes with new versions of her selves incorporated into the most recent incarnations, sometimes with the latest models being unaware of what had happened to the one just before her.

*"I promise,"* he'd told her, but he could tell she didn't believe him, and even now he wasn't sure he believed himself. That was part of why he wouldn't be in the room when they woke her up. So he sat in the living room of the penthouse he'd managed to rent under a fake name—nobody would assume a shadowy

bunch of hacker-terrorist-geneticists would be able to afford *uptown*—and let the others wake her up, waited for her to come out and sit down next to him on the couch and ask how she'd died this time.

*"Promise me you'll always make me remember what I am, too,"* she'd demanded. And she probably hadn't believed him about that, either.

# 9

//Robbie, listen.//
"What? Who?"
*Not again.*
//I'm sorry, Robbie.//
"About what?"
"Hurry up. He's starting to talk."
"It takes a second, you know."
//At least the next you won't remember that last part.//
"Why..."
*Why?*
*What?*
"Okay. Hold him steady."
"Hurry."
//CGT, CGC, CGA, CGG, AGA, AGG//

The blonde nearly shoved the operative over the cart as she grabbed at a sticky-monitor, slapped it onto the Robbie's left temple.

"Shit. There's nothing." She pulled up his eyelid.

The second operative, calmer, had attached five leads to the Robbie, professionally and quickly, and was watching on a small eye screen attached to a headband. The first operative was putting an alligator clip on the Robbie's right earlobe.

"Heart going into arrest," Operative Two reported.

"Don't fucking lose him." The blonde waved her hand in front of its face.

"What do you want me to do?" Operative One, sounding a bit panicked. Three more wires clutched in his hands as he slowly slid a lengthy needle into the base of the Robbie's skull. This was where it had shut down the last time. She could see the concentration on the operative's face, watched him chewing his lip like a fucking *seamstress*.

"Jam the fucking thing right into his brain if you have to. Give him adrenaline. Keep that heart going." She took two of the wires herself. One had a long curved needle attached to it and that one she began to thread into the edge of the Robbie's jaw, waiting to feel the connection with the vagus nerve.

"I'm telling you, there's nothing."

"There can't be nothing." The blonde felt the needle bite on the nerve. She let her breath out. Four down and the fifth was the easiest. It just got pushed into a nostril; either one would do.

"Look at his eyes," one of the men said.

She did. They weren't even rolling up in his head. They appeared blank, formless. They had the look of a screen that had never been used. "Adrenaline!" She hissed the word, knowing it was too late. This was worse. Worse than whatever lockdown he'd used on his mind last time.

"I did. Nothing. His heart's like a lump of clay."

"Jesus H." She slapped the Robbie's face. It didn't react. The wires hung limply from the base of his skull and off of parts of his face. She saw that all the muscles were slack. The body wasn't making any effort to avoid the strain of hanging from the handtubes.

"Well, I guess pack it up?"

She didn't look at either of the other two. She just stared at the Robbie, from an inch away from his face as if she could see into his brain cells. On the cart screen, the same empty image she'd seen in the tech lab, off the other dead Code.

"Whatever. Melt him. Then get me someone from Home."

The blonde walked away from Robbie's dead, cold body, wondering how a man hanging from restraints could not only stop his own heart, but keep it from being started again, and wipe every cell in his mind clean of every chemical reaction they'd ever experienced, all while not even opening his eyes.

# 10

To: Legal://Research.17A23//Marketing.22K
RE: Copyright

    :? If we could recreate the Code of a creator of an artistic work, would that resurrect the copyrights that creator holds?

**11**

He opened his eyes.

"Louis," he said. "My name is Louis."

He looked around, and saw two faces above him, one a stern-looking man whose face was still young but whose eyes seemed far older, wearing a slight frown on his face. In less time than it took to focus on the frown, Louis knew him.

"Koss," he said. "Koss Ernst."

Koss' face moved in a way that indicated the muscles were trying to smile but had perhaps forgotten how.

"Hello, Louis."

The other face, a girl, was still unfamiliar to Louis. This didn't worry him. He was used to memories taking a bit to fall into place, for his brain to learn where they all were, again this time. He was also used to people knowing him when he had not even the slightest clue who they were. And this woman looked like someone he wouldn't mind getting to know all over again.

"Who's she?" As he asked, he stared a bit at her low-cut shirt, buttoned, or unbuttoned, so as to show a significant amount of cleavage.

The question caused Koss to glance briefly at the woman, who shook her head a little. They both briefly consulted their screens. The blonde mouthed the word *incomplete*.

Louis didn't have to ask what that meant. He assumed eventually he'd catch back up and anyway how could you miss memories you didn't know you'd lost?

"She, Louis, is your girlfriend."

"So I've got a girlfriend this time?"

"Yes."

Louis looked at the cleavage again, at the girl's pretty face. "Lucky me," he said.

"Yes," she said. "Lucky you. But don't get any ideas." She looked at Koss. "So I'm through with the operatives?"

Koss shook his head. "Not yet. But it's getting dangerous. They may already know about Louis. We can't have them find out about you."

"And you are?" Louis asked the woman. He sat up, a bit shaky. He never grew used to the way his muscles felt when the only 'exercise' they'd had was being shot through with mild electric currents while bathing in a nutrient bath during the entire just-about-a-month they'd existed. It always took him days, if not weeks, to acclimate himself to the feel of his own body.

He stared down at his hands. If you grew up with your hands they always appeared to be your hands, but he remembered, almost every time he woke up, having the same thought: *I have weird hands.* His arms, muscled like a track sprinter's—lean and sculpted, long—led down from broad shoulders. His head, naturally thin-haired, had only a bit of stubble on it and would soon be clean-shaven again, once he got a chance to attend to it. His legs were powerful, even— or especially—for having never been actually used.

But attached to that body were these delicate hands with long, tapering fingers and nails that always looked manicured. The only thing to indicate that they were actually his was their coloring: a light, almost creamy brown, like the rest of him. Other than that, the hands could have been anyone's but his.

He finally stopped staring at his hands and looked back up when the woman answered him. "I'm Archie," she said.

Louis smiled at her. "Nice to meet you, Archie." He looked back at Koss. "So how did it go?"

"Not good. They were on us pretty fast. Maybe they knew we'd found him? Either way Robbie had no real chance of getting away and they got him. Now, I'm pretty sure we lost him. They grabbed him and took him to Security, anyway, and assuming they went through the usual procedures..."

Louis sat still, waiting for his mind to believe that his legs could stand up. "A complete loss?"

Koss nodded briskly. "Hopefully, it was."

Louis knew that Koss didn't mean any harm to Robbie, just that it was better if Robbie's latest round of memories weren't preserved anywhere. If those memories didn't exist, then the company didn't know any more about Robbie than their little group did.

"So we need to tell you the plan," Archie said. Louis rubbed the back of his neck.

"Gimme a second, will you?" Sometimes waking up meant muscles cramping irregularly, and he felt aches starting. But he stood up, wavering only a bit, feeling Koss and Archie grabbing his arms to help steady him. "I'm okay. Let's go. Let's go."

"We appreciate this, Louis," Archie said.

Koss, as almost always, said nothing. Louis expected the hallway of the old warehouse located near the docks, was ready to feel the chill in the air that was always there, even in summer—*Is it still summer?*—but realized they were standing in what might have been a kitchen at one point, with high ceilings and skylights up above them.

The cupboard doors had been removed and held bundles of wires, vials of amino acids and nutrient baths. The counters were covered in keyboards and monitors and there were cables winding across the floor where a table would have sat—were it an actual kitchen—and to the three large tanks, two of which had bodies in them in slightly-less-advanced stages of growth.

The third was empty, and Louis knew it was the one he'd been pulled out of. He glanced at the bodies, saw another Archie and one he didn't recognize.

Koss led him not to the conference table that had been used in the warehouse, but through a door and into a living room filled with luxurious furniture. Everything was white and plush and soft. The walls were slightly curved wherever he looked, giving the room an endless and wide feeling. The ceilings were thirty feet tall and bounded around the top with arched windows that were high enough to show only blue sky outside.

Several couches and chairs were grouped in the center of the room, with a few small screens and one larger one sitting on the table between them. Koss and Archie took seats and Louis finally did, too; his legs wanted to be up and moving around, but he didn't want to push them, yet.

The screens were repeating images of people and faces. Louis recognized in some snippets the two men who had gone in to the Gravity Sling store with Archie just before Koss had decided it was worth it to set up the shop down the mall from this latest Robbie. These clips were obviously hacked or pirated footage from any number of security screens around town, showing the men undergoing various activities.

At one point the larger screen actually showed a shot of two men and the woman entering the Gravity Sling. Louis turned his attention from the larger screen at that and watched Archie for a second to see how she reacted to the footage. If there was a reaction, Louis couldn't detect it.

Koss was looking up at the windows,

rubbing his wrist idly. He began talking. "We still need better numbers on how many Codes they've made..."

Louis didn't mind Koss' use of the word. Usually when people said *Codes* they apologized, or hesitated at least before using the word, which sometimes had a pejorative tone to it. It was that hesitation or apology that actually made it sound worse, though. The apology communicated the message that the person *did* think the word had a negative connotation.

Not Koss. He never apologized. He just talked about Codes the way he talked about everything: businesslike, and with little accommodation to society's niceties.

"But the company is getting cagier about them, even as it expands the business." He flicked a tablet in front of him and the large screen changed to show a video of workers on an assembly line.

A voice spoke softly, in some sort of Asian language, and neither Louis nor Archie could make out what was actually being said. Koss began translating, his voice barely louder than the woman's voice in the video:

"... no need to retrain your workers, and no worrying about whether they get injured or dissatisfied. In less than a month, any good worker can be brought back online, oftentimes with improved morale and performance. Ownership of genes can be obtained through a variety of consents to keep your competitors from getting your secrets. Remember, we make things, better."

Koss thumbed the sound down. "That was

intercepted by some of our bots. They've been marketing to sports leagues, too, and I believe entertainment companies, all of it very quiet, all of it very oblique. Usually it's a vague flier and then personal contact once they're assured the secret will be kept, and why would it not?"

"How about our posters?" Archie asked.

"They're getting torn down faster than we can put them up. New contacts are down. You've both been out in the field for some time, so this may come as a surprise to you: we're losing."

It did not come as a surprise to them. Koss, and the rest of their small-but-growing—growing too slowly—group were underfunded, under-technologized, and under the radar: the vast majority of people had no idea that this battle was even being fought. They knew Koss was wanted for corporate espionage, was all, and Koss had not yet taken his story public.

Nobody knew why he hadn't done that, but he hadn't, and he refused the suggestion every time it was brought up. He told the others that while this was not a one-man show, while he was not a dictator, while he couldn't control them and wouldn't try, they really, really ought not to let the general public know about the Codes. Not yet, anyway, he sometimes added.

Since almost everyone he worked with was a Code who owed their freedom, if not their existence, to Koss, they did what he asked. If privately they wondered whether they had been created by the company and liberated—after some fashion—by Koss, or if they had been created by Koss to help save others, they kept those thoughts to themselves. Some day in the future, they would be able to sit in leisure and wonder what it meant that they had been *made* rather than *just happened.* If it meant anything at all.

"What was Robbie?" Louis asked.

Archie turned away from the screen and looked at Koss appraisingly.

Koss put his hands on his head, still watching the video on replay, still mouthing the words to himself. He didn't look up at them. "I don't know," he said.

"You don't know?" Louis asked. "But didn't you write him?"

Louis, like many Codes, had come to terms with the fact that he was no longer the product of a random mixing of information, that he had been designed and replicated—six times, already! Some Codes didn't like to talk about it. Louis himself wasn't bothered by it. Much. When he thought about it at all, he realized that if he *wasn't* a Code, he'd be dead now. Five times dead.

Instead, he was still here, and now *here* was a luxury apartment somewhere—he could tell from the feel of the plush massage-carpet below his feet, if from nothing else—in the good part of town. *Beats the warehouse*, he thought.

He was looking at Archie as he asked Koss the question about writing Robbie, trying to gauge how she felt about being one of them. *I guess my memories of her were lost with the last me*, he thought. He had gathered what had happened to Louis Number 5, because on the screen a snippet had showed the blonde, the hallway, Louis falling to the ground, Robbie being taken away by security. So he tried to figure her out now. Did she mind being a Code? Did she want to be *just human?* Would she object to being described as having been written?

But just as when the blonde had come on the screens, Archie didn't visibly react.

That all flashed through Louis' mind just as Koss answered: "Yeah. Sort of. I mean, yeah I did."

"Sort of?" Louis wondered if his confusion was a result of the month-plus he obviously had been out of commission. *Was it that long?* He couldn't remember how far along this body had been when he'd been sent to deliver that screen to Robbie, the screen Koss had modified. *Of course I can't remember. That body died in that hallway and never came back here to give its memories to me.*

He realized that both number four and number five must have been made in the warehouse. How else would he remember it? He wondered how long they'd been in this hideout. Whether the Louis that died in the hallway had enjoyed coming here?

Koss sighed. "I thought maybe I recognized the code." They all *recognized* Robbie but Louis knew Koss was talking about the stuff inside Robbie's head, not his appearance. "But it was a while ago and I'd written a bunch of codes, before they knew I knew."

"So look at your notes," Louis said.

Archie stood up and walked around the couch, stretching her back. Koss stared at the muted screen, then finally smiled a half-smile. Louis recognized it as the slightly smirky look Koss got on his face when he had to tell people something unpleasant. "I'm not sure I wrote it at all."

Archie suddenly looked down at him. "Explain that," she said. They all watched on the screen as a recording showed Robbie walking into the sandwich shop where Archie sat behind the counter.

"I wrote some stuff to create new Codes."

Archie sat back down and Louis leaned forward. Koss picked at some imaginary lint on his knee.

"I wrote an algorithm to create new algorithms for Codes," he said finally, by way of explanation, "to implant not only my specific lines, but to come up with new ones along a general set of lines: codes to create new codes, to create new Codes-with-a-capital-C, each of which might have nothing, but which might have something that would be helpful to us."

"Evolution." Archie said it quietly. Her eyes were narrowed in concentration. She turned back to the screen, paused it on his face. She appeared to be trying to read his code through the screen, as if that were possible.

"Mutation." Louis nodded in agreement.

Koss just stared at the frozen face on the video. Louis wondered if Koss felt proud, when he thought of things like that. Koss had not only discovered what was happening to humanity—happening slowly, maybe at first, but with increased speed every day and all in the name of profits and control—had not only seen that, but he was fighting back against it.

As if that wasn't enough—taking on the company itself and by proxy all the corporations that would eventually make use of Codes, commodifying humanity, devolving it—Koss had, in effect, restarted the whole system by which humanity had become so great in the first place. Replacing people designed for profit and slavery with randomly-made people who might have flaws but who also might have genius!

Louis appreciated the twist on it. They were undermanned and outgunned. They stood no chance, really, of beating the company. There was no stopping the genetic steamrolling of humanity into a series of cookie-cutter human prototypes manipulated into being slaves, each model made for one particular purpose.

They were fighting a losing guerilla action, waiting for a break, and now Koss had given them that break: he had reintroduced the randomness that had been the hallmark of genetic mixing, that had helped humans move up from simple lungfish to clever apes to godlike beings who could assure their own immortality and create grown people in an apartment kitchen.

You could write a program to create perfect human beings and then copy that program over and over and over until humanity was just a series of golems, but someone like Koss would always be around to throw a monkey wrench into the works... Louis hoped.

# 12

The blonde started running, and the commotion she caused as she charged in made the people around the kiosk start running, too, but the two operatives were coming at them from different sides, closing off escape routes. Even as the crowd tried to fall back and other onlookers began paying attention, the targets were singled out. *Krzzk. Krzzk. Krzzk.* Three onlookers dropped, and the rest of the people walking through that part of the campus slowed to see why three young people had just dropped to the ground after the blonde had charged in.

She paid the crowd no attention until she tore down the poster the three targets had been posting. It showed a college-aged guy with slightly mussed hair and a winning half-grin on his face.

Emblazoned around the picture were the words:

**Maybe your memories were written by a guy paid $16.75 per hour to write them. Maybe**

that guy's last job was writing video games.
**Find Out Who You Are.**

The blonde held up the poster, slightly crumpled in her hands, and brandished it at the ten or so people who had already gathered around. Hoping nobody had fully registered or observed what had just taken place, she began the process of muddying up their memories:

"Who put this up?" she asked, her voice sounding strained and scared.

Nobody answered. They stared at her.

"Did anyone see who put this up?" the blonde asked again.

"Why?" an older man, probably a teacher at the college, asked.

"Are they okay?" a younger girl asked, motioning to the three people who laid prone on the ground.

"I don't know," the blonde said, truthfully, before switching to a smooth lie. "We were trying to get them away from this," again waving the poster "and they collapsed."

"It looked like you attacked them," the older man said.

The operatives were checking pulses. One said, "An ambulance has been called."

The blonde did not face the older man as she answered. "I was trying to get them away from this. Have you seen these? These "Find Out" posters?" A few nods. "They're dangerous. They have embedded electronics in them and they can cause seizures."

"What?" the older man asked.

A few onlookers stepped a tiny way back.

"I'm not kidding," the blonde said. "I'm with Public Health. We've been trying to track these down all over the city. So far, nearly 35 people have had near-fatal experiences with these posters. Someone thinks it's a joke, maybe, or it's part of some sort of plot or something."

"I didn't hear anything about it on the Net," a boy said.

"They don't want to encourage these sickos," another boy said, adding, "Probably."

The blonde nodded at him. "He gets it. Nobody saw who put this up?"

An ambulance was pulling up to the curb.

"I'm not sure," the older man said.

The blonde held the poster up to him. "Not sure? Take a look," she told him. The man grasped each side of the poster and was looking at it and as he did so an ambulance driver pressed something into his back.

*Krzzk.*

The man dropped, too.

Several of the people in the crowd gasped, and one of the girls looked queasy. Everyone shied away from the poster as the blonde waved it at them. "Do you see what I mean?" she said, her voice raised to pitch out beyond the immediate grouping. The operatives began picking the man up, too, transferring him to a stretcher, putting all four of the people into the ambulance, whose lights flashed silently, yellow-red-yellow-red.

More people were drawn in. The blonde took out her screen. "Anybody here have a screen?" she asked. There were nods. "I can give contact information. We need to stop whoever is doing this before more people get hurt." She crumpled the poster more thoroughly in her hand. A few screens were produced and the blonde tapped hers a few times. "I'm sending my contact information at P.H. If you see more of these posters or anyone putting them up, please let me know."

"I've seen more," one of the boys near the edge of the crowd volunteered. "They're all over campus, like ten of them."

"Show me," the blonde said. She turned to the operatives. "You," motioning to one "With me." To the other: "You go with them and help them." As the second man passed by, he whispered to her "Already wiped."

The blonde swore under her breath, turned to the boy. "Let's go get these posters."

The boy led her and the one operative off down a path that cut through the quad, surrounded by buildings that had mockups of varying ages on them. Despite the fact that every building on the college campus was the same age, or maybe because of that, the college administration had opted to set the façade-bricks on the front to mimic a wild variety of more-or-less typical university buildings.

About half had bricks-and-ivy. About a third of the others had glassy, modernistic fronts. No two appeared alike, with all of the effort hiding the fact they were walking through a set of buildings that—absent the trickery—would have looked like nothing more than a set of industrial warehouses.

Back at the kiosk the crowd stood for a few moments longer, watching the ambulance leave, a semi-circle now around an empty space previously occupied by the blonde and her actions. Then, talking amongst themselves, with more than a few heads shaking in disbelief, they began to slowly break up.

Robbie had arrived on the edge of the group just as the man had taken hold of the poster. Now he stood back and watched the ambulance leaving. After it was gone he stared in the direction the blonde and that kid and the other guy had walked off.

*Other posters?* he thought.

Robbie had never seen a poster like the one the blonde had torn down, but his brief glimpse of it as she'd waved it around had made it feel like something in him was tearing open. Now, he had the thrilling feeling that comes along with opening a present, or turning a corner in an amusement park, or waking up in the backseat of a car when you have fallen asleep on a road trip. The world around him suddenly seemed both familiar and unfamiliar, full of possibilities for amazing things. His vision seemed to widen out, somehow, things on the periphery seeming clearer than they had. He felt a little giddy.

"Find out who you are," he mumbled to himself. A man bumped into him as he stood there talking to himself, and the gruff voice telling Robbie to get moving or get out of the way brought him back only a bit. He was late for Physics, and needed to be at every lecture or he'd fall further behind. The class was already tough enough without missing it, and the midterm was coming up, but he couldn't stop repeating that phrase: "Find out who you are." He stood, his eyes closed, the breeze ruffling his hair, saying it to himself, feeling a bit dizzy, until someone else bumped into him. He opened his eyes and abruptly decided—*Fuck physics*—then started walking off in a direction perpendicular to the one the blonde was heading in with the guys. He wanted to, needed to, find a poster and see if he couldn't get more of that feeling.

Already, his head was awash in a mixture of images and scents and feelings and sounds and things even more tactile: half-glimpsed ideas of dinners at a large table, of swinging on a swingset with an older man pushing him, of driving a car

*When have I ever owned a car?*

*What makes me think that was my memory?*

*What is going on?*

He walked without noticing his surroundings across the quad, past the physics building where he was now officially missing from class and along the pathway, hardly paying any attention to anyone, so he barely realized the attractive woman and a tall, skinny black guy holding hands and walking towards him were in his way. He was hardly aware of skirting around them as he rubbed at his temples and wondered whether there would be more posters up by the student union. He was therefore quite surprised when the black guy spun around and said, "Robbie?"

Robbie heard his name but didn't stop for nearly five steps, so great was his compulsion to find another poster, the momentum in his mind carrying through to his legs. But he did stop, and turned around.

*Louis.*

The word popped into his mind.

"Do I..." he began but couldn't finish the sentence.

"Robbie!" the woman holding hands with the man—*Louis?*—said. Robbie focused on her and suddenly couldn't look away.

"Yeah..." he said, confused.

*How do I know them?*

They came up to him, stood just in front of him. The man, *Louis*, put his hand on Robbie's shoulder as though to calm him. Robbie felt like he was vibrating, between the poster and now this.

The woman inspected his face closely. Her blonde hair, close-cut and sort of spiked in a way that half-looked like it was intentional and half-looked like she'd just woken up, nearly brushed his forehead, she was so close.

*This woman kissed me, once. This woman slapped me, once. This woman and—me and the black guy, Louis, and some guy... some guy... some guy... all in a meeting*

*Koss.*

"It's you," the woman said. She looked at Louis. "I can't believe we found another one so fast."

Robbie stared at her profile. He wanted to reach out and touch her.

*What's going on with me?* he thought. Yeah, she was *beautiful,* but he'd seen lots of beautiful women and never felt compelled...

"JHC!" Louis hissed. "Not so loud ..." He looked from Robbie to the woman and back again at Robbie. Robbie barely noticed. He was watching the woman's lips move as she turned back. She saw him staring at her and they met eyes for just a second. She smiled, just a little, as though she'd figured something out about him.

*Archie,* Robbie suddenly knew her name and as he thought the name his face grew flushed. He bobbed his head, almost involuntarily, and realized that he had been about to lean in and kiss her. *Archie.* It felt like he'd said it before, softly, in the dark.

"Archie!" Robbie exclaimed, almost involuntarily.

"So you know me," she said. The smile became more full. She looked... relieved?

*Koss.*

"It's like... like opening a book, but," Robbie began, and Louis finished the sentence, speaking along with Robbie.

"—but one you once read, a long time ago."

Robbie stared at Louis. "How do I..."

*Koss.*

"Oh, shit, Robbie, we've got to run!" Archie yelled suddenly and looked over his shoulder.

Robbie looked, too, and saw the blonde and the kid and the guy—*the operative*—coming at him. His heart jumped when he saw the blonde, and not entirely out of fear, despite the look on her face: she was scowling, mouth thin, eyes narrowed. She was staring directly into his eyes and even though he understood, immediately, that she was no good a part of him wanted to wait for her to get to him. But the guy with her broke the spell. His face broke into a grin as he began sprinting towards the three of them, the kind of smarmy, too-confident look that Robbie had always instantly hated on guys like him.

*Find Out Who You Are.*

He turned back and saw Archie and had no trouble then taking off running with her—*how do I know them?*—and Louis, heading back across the quad, zigging and darting among surprised people, over women laying on their backs on the grass tanning, underneath a Frisbee game and past a group of people handing out fliers. The blonde and the operative with her kept after them with no pretense that this was anything but a chase. It was all done in silence, though. Nobody yelled to "get them" or anything like that. Robbie was right behind Archie, just ahead of Louis. He watched Archie's shoulders flex under her t-shirt. Something was bugging him, and he had to try to work it out. He threw a glance over his shoulder, trying to see the blonde, but he saw only Louis' face, serious, focused.

Here and there people caught briefly in the pursuit objected but the runners went past them so quickly the objections went unheeded if not unheard. Archie led them into a building—the physics building, Robbie noticed—and immediately turned right, then left, through empty hallways with door upon door upon door on them. Robbie and Louis were close behind.

Right again, down the hall. Robbie heard footsteps behind them. So their pursuers were in the building. The trio moved went up some stairs as the footsteps of their pursuers sounded like they were getting closer, maybe. It was hard to tell. Down the hall on the second level then right right right. Robbie realized they'd turned around and were heading back through the building almost to the way they'd come. He heard footsteps off to their right. Archie held up a finger and the three slowed, stopped, almost, turning to go quietly back down the stairs they had just come up, padding carefully to avoid their own footsteps echoing through the stairwell.

Robbie could hear the blonde and her partner heading farther off and then up the stairs again. Archie led them quickly and softly down to the first floor and back out into the quad. "Come on!" she yelled, and they ducked around the right side of the building, past hedges and shrubbery to the back where there was a loading dock area and some utility access panels.

She pulled a metal rod out of her pocket, flipped out a powerdriver, and unbolted one of the locks on the door, slipping it open. "We can get away through this," she said, and led Louis and Robbie down some dimly-lit stairs, the door shutting solidly behind them. They turned into a long, dampish corridor that Robbie thought must be used for maintenance, and began walking along more slowly, Archie pulling out her handheld and tapping at it.

"Sure you should do that?" Louis asked.

Robbie felt his feet slide a little on the slick floor below them. The hall smelled of mildew. He tried to breathe through his mouth.

"I'm not going to transmit. I need a map." Archie told Louis.

"They might be able to read reception, too."

"We have to take that chance. I'm smart but I don't know the entire freaking university underground."

They'd kept walking while this was being discussed. Archie must have found what she was looking for, as she began to give directions.

"Go over there," she said, and pointed left.

*"GO OVER THERE!" she shouted and Robbie looked at the door. The house was so old it still had wooden doors, with actual paint on them. The paint had been peeling, nicked around the doorknob from generations of people brushing it with their hands. The door to the cylinder lab had...*

*The door to the what?*

"I need to know what's going on," he said.

Archie quieted him. "Be patient. We need to get you safe, first. You're lucky we noticed you before she did. You were walking right up to her."

"What does *that* mean? Was she looking for me?" he asked.

"Yes," Louis said, just as Archie said "No."

*Great.*

*Yes, Archie said...* Robbie heard in his mind her voice, whispering *Yes*.

She was saying now, in a low voice: "She didn't know you were there. NOBODY knew you were there. But that doesn't mean she wouldn't have recognized you when she saw you. Like she did."

"Koss must have known he was here," Louis said. "He sent us here to put up those posters. He could've told us to look for him, though."

Archie didn't answer.

They continued walking through the purple glow of emergency lights, occasionally opening another door. Robbie figured they must have gone out past the quad now, if his sense of direction was any good.

"Why wouldn't he tell us?" Louis wondered.

"Why, indeed," Archie said. It was not a question.

Louis looked at her. "You didn't know, did you?"

"Me? Hardly. I know about one-tenth of what people think I know, and I'm lucky at that. Robbie here is a complete surprise to me. So far as I knew, he never made more than one at a time."

Robbie thought she sounded unconvincing. They kept tramping through the corridor, which felt unpleasantly sewer-like and was barely lit by blue access bulbs.

"Made? Who? Who's Koss?" Robbie asked. *Code* popped into his mind. "What's a Code?"

Archie looked over her shoulder at him. "You are," she said.

*"You are what we call a code," Koss said.*

Robbie remembered that somewhere in his past—

*Pasts.*

*Find Out Who You Are.*

"Where are we going? And what's a Code, anyway?" Robbie asked.

"We're going to meet Koss, to answer your first question," Archie said.

"And my second?"

Archie shook her head. "Not now."

They were at a door, the bottom of which leaked sunshine. "Think there's anyone out there?" Archie asked.

"Hard to tell," Louis said. "Let me go first."

They all hesitated for a second. Robbie tried to listen, realized how ridiculous that was. If there was an ambush waiting on the other side of this door, they wouldn't be making any noise. He felt tense. He wanted to take Archie's hand, and was amazed at himself. *Stop it*, he thought.

*I don't want to stop it*, something in him said.

Robbie held his breath as Louis turned the handle and opened the door. They stood atop a short staircase that led down to an access driveway. There were no blondes, no operatives, no security waiting for them. Instead, Robbie saw only a guy smoking some hash while leaning against an old tattered car.

"Shit," Louis said. "Hello, Chip."

Chip smiled. He brushed at his hair, a gesture that did nothing to untangle the raggedy mop that hadn't been cut in too long. He was slumpy, a bit pot-bellied, Robbie saw, in the way of guys who spend their day doing nothing much, soft rather than chubby. His jeans appeared frayed for real, and were dirty in a way that suggested Chip wanted them that way. His nose was too small for his face, Robbie thought.

"You guys are so predictable," Chip laughed.

Robbie noticed Archie looking around. He felt as though he could almost hear her saying: *If he found us they found us.* But then without further hesitation she grabbed Robbie and Louis and pulled them into the car.

"Get us home, Chip?"

Chip got into the car, too, somehow not seeming to move quickly, his motions languid, half-stoned even in his hurry. "Sure," he said, his voice drawing the word out. "Where's home today?"

Archie told him.

"There?" Chip said. "Really?"

"Really."

Chip patted the ragged dashboard. "This car's not gonna cut it down in that neighborhood. I'll get stopped ten feet in. Can you...?"

Archie was already waving him off, tapping repeatedly on her screen. "What's the tag-in? Do you have cells all over?" she asked.

Chip nodded and gave her a three-digit number.

There was a shout behind them. Robbie looked over his shoulder but didn't see anything before Louis shoved him down on the seat.

*Hey...*

*"Get Down!"* someone shouted over the sound of cylinders breaking. Then there was the crack of a wooden door, slamming first before being torn into bits. Someone was shoving him into a cubby, attaching wires to his earlobes. "I'll need you..." a voice whispered.

*What?*

The car shimmered as Chip spun the wheel and cornered sharply, getting them away from their pursuers' line of sight. Chip took another hard left, then a sharp right, getting onto a freeway ramp. As he did so, the interior of the car lost its dingy look and instead turned into something resembling fine leather. The exterior seemed to lengthen and get shinier, from what Robbie could see. The car still drove like an old jalopy, but to everyone's eyes it was a luxury cruiser befitting of their destination: uptown.

"Shit!" Archie swore. They all turned to her, but she was glaring at Chip.

"What?" Chip asked.

"Those are Real clothes, Chip?"

He looked down, his shirt unchanged, a dirty, faded rock concert t-shirt advertising some old, old group that apparently was named after dirigibles.

"Yeah," he said. "Why?"

"Who's going to believe you're driving this car?" Archie complained.

"It's a bit late for that," Chip said. "We're going to be there in ten minutes."

Archie looked over at Louis. "You'll have to drive."

"What am I supposed to do?" Chip asked. "I don't want anyone else driving my car."

"You're going to have to hide," Archie said.

"Hide?" Chip groaned.

"Yes," Archie said. "You, too." Pointing to Robbie.

As they drove they worked out the details, and Chip pulled off one exit early. They coasted to a stop and quickly switched, Louis hopping into the drivers' seat and switching his suit to a nicer one, suitable for a driver in uptown, while Archie had Chip and Robbie crouch down on the floor. "Best I can do," she mumbled.

"Farmhouse," Robbie said, aloud.

The car was winding slowly through the less-trafficked streets uptown.

"What?" Louis said.

Robbie looked up from the floor of the car, sitting next to Archie's shins, which were folded onto the seat to make room for him on the cramped floor that he knew was dusty and dirty but which appeared spotless.

"Aren't we going to a farmhouse?" he asked.

Chip stared at him. "What's he talking about?"

Robbie shook his head as though it was a snow globe. "I'm getting confused," he said. "Not a farm. Somewhere else. An old warehouse..." He tried to focus. "Or both?"

"How long did you get to look at the poster?" Archie asked.

"What? Not long," Robbie said.

*Find Out Who You Are.*

He pressed his hands to his temples.

"The farmhouse," Archie said thoughtfully. "So that's the last time..."

"The farmhouse was two headquarters ago," Louis said. "But I didn't think that Robbie had been..." he was interrupted by a slapping sound as Chip put his hand on Archie's leg, and got smacked away.

"What! I'm just trying to get comfortable here," Chip protested.

"Don't get too comfortable. I'm thinking."

*Don't get too comfortable! This is acting!*

*It didn't feel like acting, as Robbie took off Archie's shirt.*

Archie looked down at Robbie. "I've got a lot of questions for you, but we can't ask them now. Stay alive."

Louis was pulling the car into a parking garage, a doorman standing nearby on the sidewalk idly watching them. Louis gave him a tight nod. The doorman nodded back: all business, all anonymous.

The garage door closed behind them. The car stopped. It was dimly-lit, and they sat there for a second until Archie said: "OK. Nobody's coming in after us. Let's go."

Then it was out of the car, across the parking lot, into an elevator, a card put into a slot. The elevator shot up, the high-speed bypass activated by the destination, which was in the upper floors reserved—at great expense, Robbie supposed—for the elite.

*Moved up from warehouses and run-down houses in front of cornfields,* he thought and wondered what that meant.

The elevator slowly rotated to orient on the door they would open to, the card giving access only to that particular suite. The people who could stay in this building did not want to share hallways with others. The car stopped, the door slid open.

"Home again, home aga—" Louis began but his words were cut off by what they all saw.

The other three hung back, staying on the elevator, not wanting to move into the destruction that lay beyond. The doors closed halfway, then reopened, and a reminder voice asked them to please exit the elevator.

Still, they stood, staring into a room in which every single item had been not just overturned, not just broken, but demolished: furniture, shelves, books, lamps, all broken into barely-recognizable shredded components of their former selves, lampshades and armrests and cushions left in tatters just large enough to make it apparent they had once been functional items, but so torn apart that it actually hurt to look at them, even though— especially because—they were simple inanimate objects, man-made things that had been there only to serve the occupants of this suite.

*Especially because of that.*

Robbie pulled his arms into his sides. He wondered what he'd gotten himself into, and almost wished he'd gone to Physics. But Archie was standing beside him and as the door reminded them again that they had to get off he glanced over at her, felt a bit more resolve.

The elevator voice noted that a call for the elevator was waiting.

"JHC," Louis said, softly. He was the first to get off the lift, stepping gingerly into the room, feet kicking at pages of books that had been ripped asunder. It appeared that each page had been individually torn out, something that would only be done to send a message.

We. Are. Thorough.

*"We are thorough, and we will not rest,"* *they'd told him and he'd tried to get out of the* *warehouse door, but they had men there, too.*

"Koss," Louis said to the others, then, louder, out into the apartment: "Koss!"

"Louis! What if they're still here?" Archie hissed.

"Look, guys, I wouldn't have driven you if I'd known..." Chip began, and Archie pulled at his shirt suddenly and viciously.

"How did you know where to find us? Were you sent there?"

"Yeah... argggh, ugh, stop that, by Koss."

Archie stopped lifting him off the ground by his shirt.

"Koss told you where we were?"

"No. He told me how to find you."

"How..."

Chip motioned to Robbie. "He transmits."

That caused Louis to stop looking at the wreckage of the room and calling for Koss. The door again reminded them that they had to release the car, the dinging being more insistent, the countdown to auto-release starting. All three of them looked at Robbie, who felt self-conscious.

*I* what *now?*

"Let's get inside," Archie said, and shoved Chip into the room. She grabbed Robbie's arm and pulled him, too, after her. The door slid shut and they were alone in the destroyed suite.

"Explain," Archie said.

"Don't you think we should look around?" Louis asked.

"The cylinders!" Archie yelled suddenly.

*Cylinders! Eyes opening suddenly as the air freshened and he drew in oxygen for the first time, saw shapes hovering over him, felt wires poking into him, waited for his eyes to remember that they knew how to see and knew what those shapes were, waited for the cylinder to open again and admit him to this new life. Thrilling…*

Archie strode to the door that ought to have led to a kitchen, pulled it open. Her face said she didn't like what she saw beyond. Robbie and Louis reached her at the same time. Chip sat in the entry room, an uncaring look on his face.

Robbie looked over Archie's shoulder. It was not a kitchen, but a lab, or what had been a lab. He could see that much. All the things in it looked vaguely familiar. There were computers, and screens, and apparatus meant to hold test tubes, and at the opposite side of the room, about fifteen feet away, there were what looked like upended tanning beds, or what had been upended tanning beds, broken into several pieces. The floor was covered near them with a slimy-looking bluish gelatin, and in each of the three beds/tubes— *Cylinders!*—lay a body.

"They're dead," he said softly.

Archie shook her head. "They were never alive," she told him.

One of the bodies looked like Louis. That one, Robbie realized, *was* Louis, albeit a waxy-looking and dead—*never living?*—Louis. "What is all this?" he asked.

Archie turned to him. "I don't have time to explain. If we had a working computer... that would be best. I'll have to use my screen."

"Your screen?"

Archie was already tapping. As she did, her fingers sliding around, activating something, she spoke to Robbie. "I need you to remember. I think you'll know more about this than I do, right now."

Robbie tried to focus on figuring out what Archie was talking about, but Louis was in the room by then, staring down at his doppelganger for a moment, then idly picking things up to see if perhaps something was salvageable.

Nothing was, of course.

*We. Are. Thorough.*

*We make things, better!*

Robbie shook his head. Archie was still talking, half to herself. He focused on her lips, told himself that he was doing so just to help try to follow what she was saying.

"—don't know what changes Koss might have made in you. Hopefully he didn't undo..." she glanced up at him, met his eyes, looked away guiltily, back down at her screen.

His vision felt swimmy. Chip had walked up behind them.

"Can I go?" he asked.

"No," Louis said, as Archie kept talking to Robbie. "We may need your car."

"Look, I was promised payment if I tracked him," he said, motioning to Robbie, "and picked you guys up. I wanna get my reward, and head out, and wish you guys luck."

Archie ignored him and Robbie tried to. She was still talking to Robbie. "—unlock you and find out what Koss, or his program, or whatever, has *done*. He thinks it's important and I don't know why he sent you out into the world without unlocking you but he *did* and now I need to know why so we've got to get things finished. It's obviously been started. The posters will do that, but they're slow and we need to finish it up. All the *right* equipment to unlock you has been destroyed behind us and while there's more over at..." she stopped and looked at Chip.

"What?" he asked. "You don't trust me?"

In answer, Archie turned back to Robbie, as Louis pulled Chip aside to talk terms about continuing to help them.

"For now I've got some apps that might help speed things along, or at least give us a little insight into you."

"Into me?"

*Find Out Who You Are.*

"I don't have TIME for this." Archie sounded hassled, not mad. "You are a Code, Robbie. I know you're confused, but we have almost no time so I have to be blunt and here it is: you are a person created in a test tube, with your personality installed into the clone." She gestured at the bodies in the tubes. "Like a computer program, a program that doesn't even know it's a program until we tell it about itself. I don't know what yet, but there's something that's a big deal about you and..."

Archie had stopped because a green glow cast itself into the room. They all looked up to see that the door to the elevator had suddenly turned green.

It meant someone was coming.

"Shit." Chip and Louis and Archie all said it at more or less the same time, with Chip's lateness being overcome by his vehemence.

Archie grabbed Robbie and pulled him from the lab, which had only one entrance, into the front room. At the far end was a spiral staircase that led up to the second level of the suite. Next to the staircase was a door that led to other rooms on this level. She practically threw him across the room towards the spiral staircase.

"Upstairs!" she hissed at him.

Robbie didn't bother asking why he had to go upstairs. He just ran, as fast as he could, to the spiral stairs and was halfway up them when the elevator doors opened and the concussion blast resounded with a hollow thunderous boom throughout the room, picking up everything in a shockwave of sound and throwing it. What was left of the furniture was further upended, the people in the room, Chip and Louis and Archie, were all flung outwards from the elevator doors and the spiral staircase was knocked sideways.

Robbie was pushed down onto the stairs, face first, his nose cracking and forcing tears into his eyes. As he stood, it was already spouting blood and hurt horribly, hurt exactly like he figured a broken nose would hurt.

"Run!" Archie yelled and pulled something from her belt. Robbie figured it was a gun. It wasn't. It was a screen. Chip and Louis were already getting up as the elevator doors closed and the lights went out. "They'll be up here in a minute; they're probably on the level below," Archie said. "We've very little time."

"Didn't need to tell us," Chip said as he shoved Robbie further up the stairs. Archie began running up after them, too, and they all reached the upper level as the elevator door again turned green.

Robbie turned left into the bedroom, Archie right behind him, Louis and Chip heading the opposite direction as the whirr of projectiles came from behind them, shots *pinging* off of walls and ricocheting around the lofted area, voice shouting, the bedroom door closing behind them

*…the bedroom door closing behind them, Archie leaning in. "Don't get ideas, the cameras are watching."*

*Find Out Who—*

"I'm bleeding." Robbie put a hand up to his head.

"Just your nose," Archie said. She was pushing against a window, as hard as she could, staring out down below as she got it open.

"No, my head," he told her.

Archie turned towards him. The screen she'd carried up was pressed up to her head, now. "What?" she asked.

"My head... I got hit by..." he stopped as a pounding on the door began, voices shouting.

"Come here," Archie said, and pulled at him. "How bad is it hurt? Let me see?"

Robbie felt his head, realized she was right: his nose was bleeding, too. "I don't know how bad it is."

She stared intently at him, the screen still pressed against a part of her temple. He could see it.

::**LOAD**:: it said.

—*You Are.*

There was the sound of a concussion grenade again and the door blasted off its hinges to shatter against the far wall.

"It'll have to do," Archie said, pulling against him. She pressed the screen into his hand. Robbie saw that unlike many screens, this one had little metallic pads on the end that had been pressed to her temples. "Try to land on me."

"What?" he asked, too late as she grabbed at his shirt and flung herself backwards out the window at the same time as two men in street clothes burst into the room, projectiles pinging all over the place.

Robbie felt himself pulled out into the open air, one hand clutching at the screen Archie had handed him, the other hand waving wildly as Archie started to fall down to the street below dragging him with her.

*This was her plan?*

Robbie felt himself momentarily hang there, his momentum not yet starting downward but still outward.

Robbie saw Archie fall further, her eyes staring back at him.

*She doesn't know I love her* he thought, as he stared at her eyes.

*"Don't get ideas," she said again but gave in to his putting a hand behind her neck, pulling her closer...*

Robbie felt a hand grab his ankle

He felt his body slam into the side of the building.

Below him, receding towards the ground, Archie's stare conveyed enough anguish to practically dig into his mind. Her desperate gambit had not worked. They had him and she was going to die.

*One of us has to live.*

He clutched the screen she'd given him as the two men tried to better their grip on him and pull him back into the building, a process that took long enough for him to see Archie fall nearly all the way to the ground.

He was back in the room, then, spared the sight of Archie's body actually hitting the pavement. He was sweating and still bleeding profusely from the nose and less so from the wound on his head. The two operatives pushed him roughly down to the floor and then looked out the window and shook their heads, mumbling about a mess. From outside of the room Robbie could hear men yelling, he assumed at Louis and Chip, to lie still.

He blinked a few times and looked up at the far wall. A poster hung there. It had been hidden behind the swung-open door when he and Archie had entered. On it a group of people stared out at him with serious expressions, overlaid with the words:

"It's not deja vu. It really has<br>happened before."

*Find Out Who You Are.*

He felt like something broke open inside his mind.

*College /Mom and dad / Swingset / Girlfriend /* **What-was-her-name?** */ Military / Laptop / Coffee-shop / Man-with-glasses / What-was-his-name? / Sister / I-had-a-sister / I-had-a-mom-and-dad / Why-did-I-never-think-of-my-mom-and-dad-before? / High-school football team / Maria / Hardware store / Pancakes! I like pancakes! / Sunset / Sunrise / January 14 /* **Noodle soup** */ Popcorn at the movies / Archie, I love you / Vacation in the Caribbean / Drill sergeant sitting on my back while I do pushups / Being shot at / Being shot at / Being shot / Running down a dark alleyway / Christmas morning I got a puppy! /* **Why-did-I-never-think-of-that-puppy?** */ Waking up in a brightly lit room / Playing the violin / Trees all around him a tent—camping? / Days / Nights / Afternoons / Tropical fish in a tank / Braces / Waking up in a brightly lit room / Barbecuing hamburgers by the lake / Taking an exam /* **If they capture you tell yourself this and you will die.** */ Waking up in a brightly lit room*

Robbie reached up and grabbed the leg of one of the operatives as he turned around, pulled on it, and the man wobbled a bit as Robbie spun towards him, digging his teeth into the man's thigh, biting right through his khaki pants. The man howled and his companion turned back, away from the pile of Archie below in the street to see their quarry seemingly eating his coworker, and before a gun could be brought to bear, Robbie had kicked at the second man and sent him stumbling backwards.

He pulled the first man to the ground and grabbed that man's gun. A quick pull of the trigger and a projectile shot right through the man's ears, sending blood spatter all across the room. Robbie glanced in the direction of the shot, saw the poster throbbing in his eyes, seemingly strobing.

*Damn, they work too slowly. Have to tell Koss*, he thought, and then choked as the operative behind him grabbed him by the neck.

"Don't want to have to kill you," this one grunted.

Robbie pulled and struggled at the strangling arm just enough that the operative forgot Robbie was holding a gun, too, forgot it right up until Robbie jabbed it right into man's eye and pulled the trigger. The projectile went in but didn't break through the back of the skull. Projectiles were made like that: get into a body and rebound again and again off anything harder than skin.

His shot through the other man's head must have been randomly, perfectly aligned to go straight through, Robbie thought. The shot into the second man's brain was doing what it was supposed to do, the kinetic energy of the projectile being almost perfectly preserved by each rebound off the man's skull, shredding his brain inside.

Projectiles took a *long* time to slow down and stop rebounding. Robbie knew. He was already standing up as the second man dropped, goo coming out of his eye socket. He heard voices from outside the bedroom door telling the men in here that the scene was secure, asking if they'd gotten *the quarry.*

He looked down at the dead assailants. Quickly reaching into their pockets he found what he was hoping had been there—a small stick about the size of a cigarette lighter. He pressed the top of it, three times, until a number appeared on the side: 2. He thumbed the top once more, the number changed to 1, and he flicked the switch, flinging the concussion grenade through the bedroom door immediately and ducking down.

The thunderclap nearly deafened him but as soon as it was over he was running out onto the balcony firing his gun wildly around and diving for the other bedroom door. He sat up to peer cautiously back out at the scene below, which showed him three other corporate security guys ducking behind furniture as the fifteen or so projectiles he'd fired pinged around the room. When they saw him, they began firing, too, and he flattened himself out, taking careful aim at them and trying to pick them off.

*This wasn't what I was made for.* He knew that was true, but he had to get out of here to do what he *was* made for, one way or the other, and he hoped that Louis and Chip would survive, but couldn't guarantee their safety either way.

*Anyway, they can come back.*

He thought of the screen he'd tucked into his shirt that held Archie, who would—if he could do it—remember her plan but never remember what it had felt like to fall ten stories knowing all the while the plan hadn't worked.

*But it was a stupid plan, she should've just shown me the poster.*

*"If you get caught say this and you'll die."*

*He is meant to die rather than be captured but also meant to be captured.*

*I am?*

Robbie wished he could make sense of the various *hims* talking to him, but there was no time. The unlocking would have to proceed at its own pace, and besides, the ruckus in the suite was dying down. Even projectiles can't maintain energy forever.

"Come out. We've got your friends" someone shouted from below, outside the room.

"You'll have to come in and get me." Robbie snuck a peek out, saw two of the men holding Louis and Chip, while the third stood behind the human shields. He saw that the elevator door was green. Someone else was coming?

"We're not that stupid," the man said. "You've got no choice but to come with us."

"I've got plenty of choices." But he knew he didn't. If he was getting out of here it was either after they were all dead, or as a captive.

Or with him dead, and all of *this* time around lost.

*"Even if there doesn't seem like there's anything to save, every life you have is worth remembering."*

*"Koss, that should be on a birthday card!"*

*Laughter, the sound of pats on the back, a glass clinking. People liked him!*

The elevator door opened.

Koss Ernst stepped out.

"He won't come," one of the men said. "Maybe you should talk to him?"

Robbie, Louis and Chip all stared in disbelief.

"Koss?" Louis said.

Koss turned towards him. "Yes, Louis. It's me."

Robbie tried to watch Koss while at the same time keeping an eye on the corporate operatives. Two were still holding Louis and Chip, while the free one had edged a bit towards the stairs while still keeping Robbie's friends in between Robbie and himself.

"What are you doing here?"

"It's fine, Louis. This is part of the plan," Koss said.

Robbie's mind flickered through hazy memories of Koss. *Not all back yet.* But he seemed right. *Didn't he?*

*Come on. Come on. Posters are* way *too slow. I need the rest of my mind.*

A flicker of a response ran through him as he thought that last part:

*Not yet* it said.

"*This* is part of the plan?" Louis asked.

Koss nodded to the operatives. "You don't have to hold them like that." The men let Louis and Chip go. Koss patted Louis on the shoulder. "Plans within plans, Louis. Plans within plans. They are smart and well-organized and wealthy. We have to be better at 2 of those 3 things at the least, wouldn't you agree?"

*Plans within plans. We can't outspend them, so we have to outsmart and outorganize them.*

Robbie couldn't place where they'd been when he'd heard Koss say that. He hadn't known, then, where in that nestled set of plans he fit. He didn't now, either, not exactly, but was starting to feel like he understood. But only just barely.

*Come on.*

Louis nodded, still looking wary.

"Look, can I just go?" Chip asked.

Koss shook his head. "Not yet. Not just yet, Chip. We've got a stop to make."

"Koss, I'm not one of your culties. I'm a free agent. I signed on to pick some people up. I brought them here. I got my freaking eardrums popped a bunch of times and nearly took a ping through the face, and I would like to get back to my business, please."

Koss looked up at Robbie, where he still lay in the doorway, gun at the ready. They met eyes.

*It's not him.*

Robbie wanted to yell out. But what good would that do? The odds were terrible, and he had to leave this apartment. He knew that, knew it with a certainty that he could feel in every cell of his body.

*Naturally.*

Whoever *this* Koss was, Robbie had to go with him, which meant that Robbie had to stay alive. He understood those things.

But he didn't want to.

If he had to go, he certainly didn't want to make it easy.

"Not just yet, Chip," Koss was saying.

"Where are we supposed to go?"

Koss had still not looked away from Robbie, who kept staring right back..

"To the greenhouse," Koss said softly.

*It's not him.*

//There's no better time.//

//There's no other way.//

*Shut up.*

Robbie stood up and dropped the gun.

"Okay, let's go," he said.

//Are you sure that's smart?//

*No, I'm not.*

//You're just voluntarily...//

*Any better ideas?*

Robbie shook his head.

*It's not as seamless as they think it is.*

//It's not, really.//

*I'll tell you one thing, Koss. If I get through this, we are improving those fucking posters.*

The memories never quite meshed anyway, always leaving you feeling almost like there were more than one of you. But this was the first time he'd gone through this process *slowly.* Every moment he could feel more lights coming on in his mind, but it was all still so confusing. More and more each moment he remembered bits of his past—pasts?—and he was starting to understand what it was he had to do, was *meant* to do, but even as all that went on he had to feel his way through this situation. While trusting that his mind would put itself together into a single entity comprised of multiple existences.

The password for their group, one time, had been a joke of sorts, that Koss had later made into one of the activation posters:
**Q: How do you know you're talking to a Code?**
**A: They never use first person.**


Robbie went downstairs, hands up, until Koss told him he could relax. "Plans within plans. You're among friends." That almost made Robbie doubt for a second. *Plans within plans.* He sounded so much like *Koss.* And Robbie couldn't be sure that this feeling that he wasn't looking at the *real* Koss wasn't just some sort of weird lag from the way he was activating. After all, a half-hour ago or so, he hadn't known who Koss Ernst *was*, had still believed himself to be a freshman on a college campus, flunking physics.

He could feel his mind turning over and over, integrating everything that he knew from every time he had been. *Maybe it's just that? Maybe this really is Koss and I'm just... not me yet?*

//No.//

They left the old headquarters behind. The screen that Archie had given Robbie was laying on the floor of the bedroom, next to the gun Robbie had abandoned.

*I loved her, once.*

*I loved her, every time.*

A flood of memories of Archie had washed into him. He made sure he did not look back up in the direction of the bedroom, the screen he'd left, as they got onto the elevator. He wondered how quickly he'd have to be back here to get it, whether it would be here when he got back. It worried him, since he had no clue as to whether whatever memories she'd managed to save into that screen were all that was left of her.

# 13

Koss lay slumped against the closet door, listening to the sounds fading away, the elevator door seal. He did not move for as long as he could bear, not so much because he was afraid of being found, but because he could not stand the amount of pain motion caused.

Eventually, though, he reached up, teeth clenched and eyes squished shut, sweat beads breaking out on his forehead, and grabbed the closet door handle. He pulled it and the door swung open. He collapsed out, gasping, onto his side into the bedroom. The furniture here was torn apart, too, shredded first by Security men from the company and then just now by multiple projectiles. Bits of wood and cushion and cloth formed heaps and the walls showed smears that might have been blood.

He tried to focus his eyes, saw the doorway impossibly far away. The door then the balcony then the stairs then through the kitchen then...what?

The lab would never be left in working order.

He was going to die, that much was sure.

Or, this body was.

A computer, he needed a computer.

He rubbed at his lips and looked again.

The door. A gun. A screen.

One of *his* screens, the ones they'd upgraded to download the most recent memories, the new ones. One of the ones that could take the basic code stored elsewhere and upgrade it. They'd improved on the company, in this area as in others. Why download the entire brain of a Code when you already had most of it in your mainframe? Just get the new stuff and the next version of whoever it was would remember everything. He'd wired together some prototype screens that would do just that. He was good at that kind of thing. That type of innovation was hardwired into him.

*And those types of jokes come too easily,* he thought.

He tried to push himself up on his elbows, ready to crawl, and howled with pain as his abdomen, which had been ripped into by at least three projectiles rebounding off walls before hitting him, wrenched and heaved. He knew that inside him, his intestines and kidneys and liver and stomach, probably, were nothing so much as a mush, beginning already to leak out through the tiny holes where the projectiles had entered.

He couldn't imagine why they hadn't taken his body with them. If he hadn't blacked out, they might have. They must not have believed they could get anything from the corpse they thought he was.

He pulled himself a foot. The screen. He could still save himself.

His mind shrieked with the agony of dragging a sack of fluids that used to be a body behind him. Tears filled his eyes.

*That was my sister.*

It was the last thing he remembered yelling when he'd called up Thompson on the phone, the last time he'd talked directly to anyone at corporate, before he'd gone underground. The memory was clear as day in his mind, always front and center, flashed into his very personality. It was what drove him forward. He loved technology. Loved advances. Loved the idea that he'd created a path towards someday getting rid of psychoses, of ending genetic diseases, of curing *every debilitating disease ever*, of making people capable of living for as long as they wanted to. He'd loved every second of it in a way that felt visceral to him, almost unreal.

And then he'd seen his sister, resurrected without his knowledge, walking down the hallway, and he'd realized that the company would have no interest in just allowing anyone to use this technology. The company would use it for profit, of course. The company would restrict access to it, warp the idea, make it into something terrible, something that would cause your own sister to rise from the dead and then walk by you in the hallway without ever even registering your presence.

Maybe the fact that the company would

use his creation as a way of destroying humanity's essence would have eventually caused him to do something about it, but seeing Archie's blank face, her pretty eyes staring blankly at him when he'd confronted her, her blonde hair grown out and pulled into a ponytail that didn't seem like her at all, seeing his own sister not recognize him and shove him out of the way, that had catalyzed him like nothing else could.

*That was my sister!*

But they were all somebody's sisters, somebody's brothers, somebody's friends, lovers, they'd all been his friends and lovers, too. Nobody had the right to just *steal* another person.

*Nobody.*

His hand, ahead of him, was coated in blood. Appropriate.

*How can you use the same technology you condemn to fight them?*

*I don't condemn the technology. I don't. I love the technology. I just don't want it used against people's will. Not for these purposes.*

*Do you ask each Code if they want to be brought back?*

He hadn't. Not at first.

They were all friends and lovers and sisters and brothers, and God only knows what his sister was doing right now, somewhere—all his sisters! How many of them were there, now? The company was obviously still making them. He'd seen her himself. At least he had *permission* to...

He shook his head with pain. Where was Archie now? He hadn't heard her voice as the others had left. Would she survive? He'd taken precautions, he knew. *Plans within plans.* She'd doubted that he'd keep her alive. She shouldn't have.

*Do you ask them if they want to feel...* he cut off that thought. Unproductive. He crawled forward another half-foot, collapsed. He clenched his jaw.

He'd started asking them before they were properly awake, "Do you want to be awake?" If they said no, he didn't wake them but erased their code, forever—he hoped, forever at least from his own systems—so that they could die properly.

He'd *started* asking them. But *plans within plans.* He'd had to set it up so that he couldn't ask, and hope that the whole thing worked. He hadn't been able to write the program himself, at all. Clever as he was— almost as if he'd been *made* clever, he realized now, and felt a bit like a veil was pulled away suddenly—clever as he was, the programming was beyond him. So he'd set up a program to write the program, to keep at it, trying new permutations until it came up with one that could actually do what they needed to do.

"Steal... fire," he said to himself, before realizing that he'd spoken aloud.

Of course, it wasn't perfect. The ones he still asked about being made again weren't always able to make the best decision. Codes that were created without new memories from their last incarnation were operating on uncertain, or incomplete, information, when they decided whether to live—again—or go away.

Go away. *Die.*

He was nearly to the screen. He wondered how much longer he had.

*I would like to wake up again*, he told himself. *So it doesn't matter if they ask me.*

Another foot or so. He felt liquid under his nose, touched it, came away with blood. He had tunnel vision, now.

A foot stepped in front of his very, very narrow field of vision. Trembling, he looked up. Blood dripped from his nose as he stared at himself.

"Thinking you'd like to save yourself?" the undamaged, able-to-stand version of him said. "Tsk. I thought we were opposed to that kind of thing."

The Koss Ernst on the floor watched as the Koss Ernst who was capable of standing picked up the screen Robbie had left behind and studied it, while the other version of himself died on the floor at his feet.

# 14

"The Koss Ernst you know," shouted Koss into the microphone before the pilot got the volume adjusted on their headsets, the sound of the helicopter rotors being too loud to talk over, "is but one of many, many, many Koss Ernsts roaming the world."

The company's grounds sailed by below them, the helicopter flinging itself forward in that way a helicopter had to, fighting to keep in the sky in the first place, every second a battle. Helicopters as a form of transportation were so ridiculous that they only emphasized how important you had to be to use such an inefficient mode of travel, and each second you spent in one served only to demonstrate that principal: *we have energy and effort sufficient to spare enough to fling a pile of metal into the sky in the most awkward way imaginable, and keep it there.*

They'd left the city behind and were over

the warren of buildings and research labs and hangars and dry-docks and launch pads that made up the bulk of corporate operations.

Koss stared at them as they took his statement in. "I know this," he went on, "because I am one of them, of course."

Louis shook his head. "I thought you were going to say you *are* him."

"I am not him and I would not have claimed that I was him, for the simple reason that first, you would not believe me." Below them, a series of small explosions in different colors—green, blue, yellow—was bursting in a field. Robbie tried not to have his attention diverted by them. "And second because there is no him."

"Huh?" Chip said, finally displaying an emotion other than sullen boredom. His repeated *I'm just a freelancer* had failed to get him out of this helicopter ride to...what? Interrogation? Probably. Death? Just as probably, Robbie figured.

*Not quite for me, though.*

*//Not yet guys.//*

*I know.*

"There is no Koss Ernst, not in the sense that you think there was once a man who was named Koss Ernst and who once worked for us here on the Campus and who was a brilliant bioprogrammer who was figuring out how to genetically engineer microbes to transfer retrovirus capability to human red blood cells when he suddenly realized that a quirk of his experiments was that you could literally encode anything onto a gene and grow it. Not in the sense that you think he then stayed up night after night after night, not leaving his lab for thirteen consecutive weeks, until he had worked out all the kinks and had come up with a way to clone human beings, precisely, and include in that clone their memories and personalities."

*"I didn't do it for that purpose, at first,"* Koss said one time, eating a cinnamon crunch scone, a piece at a time, picking it apart with his fingers. *"I did it so they could send troops into battle and not worry if they died because they'd keep their memories and the troops would come back and could choose to forget the entire war if they wanted."*

*::This is bullshit, you know.::*

*//Is it?//*

*How many of me are me?*

The helicopter dipped towards one of the buildings. From outside, it looked like a massive greenhouse. It was a giant structure, made almost entirely of windows through which they could see, even from this height, people walking to and fro amidst rows of computers and neat lines of tubing and countertops containing microscopes, scanners, slides. This hive of activity was surrounded by lots and lots of tanks standing in silent rows around the edges of the building. The tanks held even more people— well, *not* people, not yet.

*So, it really is a greenhouse.* Robbie thought the name might be some sort of inside corporate-speak. He found it amusing that the place where all this actually occurred, the heart of the company's program, was so transparent. Someone in the company had a sense of humor.

One of the apparently many Koss Ernsts continued talking. "That Koss Ernst—or any particular Koss Ernst, never existed in the way you think he did. He's a myth, an urban legend."

"Created by who?" asked Louis, as they came into the helipad atop the greenhouse.

"Created by Koss Ernst, of course," said Koss Ernst.

*But not **the** Koss Ernst.*

*Unless he is?*

"I don't get how this is supposed to be believable," said Louis, while Chip just looked cross. The helicopter landed, and Koss motioned for them to take off their headphones, to join him. It looked like an invitation.

The three armed guards standing outside the door somewhat dampened the friendly effect.

They ducked out of the helicopter, walked dizzyingly across the translucent roof of the greenhouse trying not to be too unnerved by the activity below, all those people and computers re-creating and perfecting personalities to be implanted into the clones. Once their twenty-eight day growth period was completed, they would be subjected to the twenty or so hours it took to have electrical impulses mimic a lifetime of activity. This got their bodies ready to actually live a life that appeared to have begun at conception but which really began here, on Campus.

{Or sometimes in one of the labs Koss Ernst—}

//But not **the** Koss Ernst?//

*Shut up.*

{—set up.}

A door lifted, opening onto a staircase which led them down the back way, away from the greenhouse with its brightly sunlit modern horrors; upon reflection Robbie realized that even as big as it was, the greenhouse was too small to be a production facility, it had to be a lab where they tested out new varieties —

//Of you.//

;;Of me, yes.;;

—of Codes.

There would be other places where people were created, as if on an assembly line, to their customers' specifications. People who would never know that they were created, who might imagine themselves to have lived lives, raised children, fallen in love, but who would never have a chance to do so. People who would find themselves so dedicated to their terrible jobs as miners or secretaries or laborers that they never even bothered to go home, never developed hobbies, never got distracted at all from what they had been *grown* to do.

//People like you.//

*Like me, yes.*

*But different because they wouldn't have ever had a real life.*

Silence in his head at that one.

The stairway was depressingly industrial. For all the menace of the company's abilities to outspend and out-think and out-market and finally, out-gun, all its competition. Including not just small fries like Robbie and

Koss Ernst—
//—but not the—//
*Stop it.*
—for all that might and wealth and excess, the company couldn't be bothered to do more than create metal staircases.

Robbie didn't know *why* that depressed him. It just did. There should have been something more sinister here. A tube that would shunt them down into the bowels of the earth. An escalator that would carry them inexorably to their fate. Not just some regular old stairs.

Clank, clank, clank down the stairs, guards behind them. Koss, then Louis, then Chip.

//That's not an accident.//
*Hmmm?*
Then Robbie, then the guards, in order, single file down the stairs.

Robbie felt like the buzzing in his brain was dying down, the way soda will stop fizzing eventually and relax back into a glass that looks calm, but if you peer at it you can see little bits of it still jumping around on the surface.

Koss Ernst kept talking while Robbie focused on Chip, now.

"...point is that the company would like very much to get people to accept Codes, but they're not going to do that on their own, now, are they? The original idea was to use them primarily in things like wars or for exploration or dangerous jobs like mining, so that people could do that kind of job and they could work until they retire—

*"I mean, somebody has to do these things right?" Koss had looked up at the rest of them. Robbie had been listening while he watched Archie play with an earring, the dangling triangle glinting in the low light of the bar. Louis had responded with something earnest, reassuring.*

"—at which point they could simply reload their memories into a younger Code and not have to remember 30 years of treacherous dull work or have post-traumatic stress disorder. You can see it was a very noble idea."

"Huh," Louis snorted.

Chip looked back at Robbie and, seeing himself being examined, nodded and raised an eyebrow.

Robbie nodded back. Chip had been the first off the helicopter, the first to the door. How had Louis gotten in front of him? Were they spreading out to make sure that he and Louis were separated? He searched his memory—memories—for Chip but had precious little to mull over. However many incarnations he was in this body, not many of them had dealt with Chip.

How many was he?

He remembered at least two elementary schools in two very different parts of the country, apparently, because he had memories of Christmas concerts and only one of them had snow outside, the other was scorching hot.

"...the military," Koss Ernst was going on "Had to wreck everything, trying to commandeer the technology for soldiers and place it under martial jurisdiction."

*Who was he kidding? The military? Like anyone believed in that.* Robbie was only half-listening now. In his mind, he imagined a city lighting up as the night fell, building after building beginning to glow. That was what his mind felt like. He was watching Chip, feeling his way through the various personalities that were *him* and trying to sort through what he *knew* versus what he had *lived.*

"...she hit on the idea of making it seem as if the Codes were some sort of group of people that needed protection—a set of folks who hadn't wanted to exist and who hadn't asked to exist and were created by a corporation to serve its own ends. Basically, she was going to viral market computer-programmed clones and make people want to protect them, to see them as something cool and desirable and loveable and vulnerable, something stolen from humanity. It was almost genius. Which is how I came to be born: Koss Ernst, the genius who came to regret his own creation."

They were at the bottom of the stairway, and Robbie realized they'd walked down far longer than it ought to have taken for them to get to the first floor of the greenhouse, which had been only 3 or 4 stories tall. He'd been only half-able to follow this Koss' story, some of which he felt like he knew already. It wasn't so much like having amnesia as it was like having a computer slowly load up. Everything was there, and you knew it was there, but you had to wait for it to be accessible to fully use it.

The staircase let into a long hallway, along which doors were set at regular intervals. The doors were the usual, alterable doors that right now were opaque but which could appear translucent. They were really just door-sized screens with simple camera mounts on each side. Here and there people in lab coats walked. Koss turned right and stood there, stopping Louis, as Robbie and Chip filed into the hallway, too.

"We're heading that way," Koss said, pointing.

"What's down there?" asked Louis.

Robbie looked over his shoulder. "More doors," he said.

//Remember what to say in a pinch, Robbie.//

*I got it.*

He hoped there was enough time, hoped more that he wouldn't have to worry about it at all.

"Right," said Koss. The guards now came into the hallway and stood between Koss and the rest of them, Chip, Robbie and Louis very apparently prisoners, now.

"Let's go," Koss said, and one of the guards gave a nudge to Robbie, who started walking, then raised his hands above his head.

"There's no need for that," Koss said.

"Why not? I'm a prisoner, right?"

*Don't be a prisoner.*

{You have to be a prisoner.}

//If you do it right//

"Not necessarily."

"That's not encouraging."

"You may be given some freedom, but we just have to guarantee something, first."

"Guarantee what?" asked Louis.

"That you're not going to blow up," Koss said, completely seriously.

*Is that possible?*

//They have no idea what you are.//

Robbie was only beginning to suspect, himself.

The guards separated them, lining each up in front of one of the doors down the hall, spread between them. Koss watched as they did this. Robbie looked from Koss over to his right, where Chip stood. Louis' door was opened and Louis sullenly went inside. Robbie's door opened.

"Make him go in first," Robbie said, motioning towards Chip.

"What? What the fuck, man?" Chip asked.

"You're with them, aren't you?" Robbie asked Chip.

"Not at all," said Koss. Robbie looked back at him.

//That's just what he would say.//

"That's just what you would say," Robbie told Koss. "But put him in the cell. Then you and I will talk."

Koss smiled. "This isn't a cell," he said.

Robbie looked back inside the room ahead of him. There was a sort of hitch on the floor and some sleeves protruding from the ceiling.

"Not the way you're thinking of it," Koss went on. "We're not going to hold you here as a prison, or anything like that. We're just going to immobilize you until we can download you and analyze your code."

//That's what we want.//

Robbie swallowed and hoped that his face didn't look hopeful.

*It is?*

//It is.//

A part of him knew they needed more time, still. *The posters are too slow, Koss.*

He looked back at Chip. "I still want to see him go in first."

"What does it matter, Robbie, if Chip is a double agent?"

"Hey—" Chip tried to interject.

"We could, after all, put him in the room and then put you in and then let him out." Koss ignored Chip.

"Look, I'm not—" Chip began.

But Robbie looked at Koss instead and said, "Then kill him."

"Hey, man!" Chip sounded pleading. Koss smiled more broadly.

"I like you, Robbie," he said. "We've been hoping to get an activated copy of you."

"Have you?" Robbie asked.

{I wonder why?}

[Is it possible he knows?]

Another one.

Robbie glanced over at Chip. It was *entirely* possible the company knew everything every Koss knew.

He felt…almost there.

"But I'm not going to kill Chip," Koss said. "At least until we can download him."

"That's crazy," Chip said, off on Robbie's right. "I'm not a fucking Code."

//So far as you know!//

"So far as you know," Robbie and Koss each said, almost simultaneously.

Chip was shoved into the room, and from inside the room Robbie heard the guard tell him—as Louis' guard had—to put his arms above his head, slip them into the sleeves. Further down beyond Koss, Robbie could see techs, armed with screens and something on a cart, entering the hall. They paused when they saw that not everybody was in the rooms, that the doors were not closed.

"That's enough, now, Robbie. Perhaps you and I will get to talk again," Koss said. "But first I have to see just how dangerous you are."

"No more dangerous than you," Robbie said.

"That remains to be seen. I tend to be quite the rogue genius, and there are a lot of versions of me. I would say the same about you but the truth is, we've never gotten an activated Robbie yet."

//So it's true: he made way more than the one at a time he promised.//

*"... and the other thing is that they make dozens of them, dozens upon dozens of basically just robots made of organs instead of processors—guys they've cloned and coded to get them to be simply automatons made out of flesh, and I think that's wrong, wrong, Wrong!"*

*The beer stein pounded on the table until the handle broke off and they all laughed, involuntarily because laughing was better than picturing a future in which humanity was created the way vacuums and computer games were. Outside, a flock of geese quacked in the empty fields.*

*Koss. Koss. Fighting fire with fire. And I'm the spark, I bet.*

"And you won't get one now. I won't let you download me," he said.

*That's what they expect me to say.*

//Buy time.//

"We'll see."

*You will see.*

Robbie stepped into the room, one foot, the second foot, and then as quickly as he could dove backwards back out, stumbling over his feet and into Koss, taking Koss down with him, before the guards could taze him. The two rolled over, with Robbie coming up on top, his hands digging into Koss' throat. Koss' face was already turning red with the exertion of trying to breathe. Robbie looked up at the guards.

"Back off or I break his neck!" he shouted, but he knew they wouldn't—he was a Code, and Koss was a Code, and nothing about a Code mattered if you could get to its brain within about a minute of the last heartbeat, even longer maybe if you kept the body full of current. The tazers hit him just as he broke Koss' neck.

*That's what they expected me to do.*

//Good work.//

He blacked out.

# 15

Below the burning building, Koss Ernst stared up, sunglasses reflecting the flames licking out of the top four floors. The explosion had been entirely unexpected. He was glad he hadn't lingered to see if any other equipment beyond the one screen he'd picked up was still workable.

He didn't know if it was a booby-trapped version of some Code—there were Codes that would explode if the right word was said to them—or if it was simply that there had been damage to some power supply or maybe just a shitload of explosives left behind by the corporate goons who had messed up the place.

Whatever it was, he'd just barely survived. The crowd continued to stare at the firefighters' efforts: hovering helicopters spraying foam designed to dampen the fire and stabilize the building, ladders being clamped to the lower levels to help people get out—the elevator shaft had been burnt out by the explosion which had thrown Koss out across the lobby as he'd left the elevator. Koss slowly pushed his way back through the crowd, murmuring "excuse me" and "pardon" as he bumped into people, but through the whole crowd he never fully turned his face towards anyone.

Each person slid out of his way, one at a time, and he was nearly to the vacant edge of the sidewalk up near the building where he could turn and walk slowly away, drawing as little attention to himself as he could. But then one man didn't move.

"Excuse me," Koss said. He backed again, using a bit of elbow. The person still didn't move. "Pardon," Koss said, a little more loudly. He looked over his shoulder, daring eye contact, and saw a Robbie.

"Whatcha got there, Koss?" The Robbie asked.

"Shut up!" Koss hissed. A few people turned their heads to see who had made the unexpectedly audible hissing noise, and Koss turned back forward, gaping slack-jawed up at the building with the rest of them in an effort to blend in.

"The screen, I mean," the Robbie said. "Although you knew that."

"Back up. This isn't the place to talk about it."

"You're right. The place to talk about it would have been in some sort of secret location, a headquarters, maybe, where we could plan without anyone else being privy to our councils and come up with an idea to help fight the power, right?"

"Right..."

A few more people appeared to be listening to this conversation.

"But you blew it up, didn't you, Koss?"

"Hey, I didn't—" Koss began, but a woman turned towards them both.

"Are you saying he blew this building up?" the woman asked.

*Nice time for people to start fucking caring about their world* Koss thought.

The Robbie turned towards the woman. "That is exactly what I am saying," he said. "Would you mind calling the police, ma'am?" The Robbie reached out and grabbed Koss' arm, holding it tightly at the elbow. Koss glared at him. With his other arm, the Robbie handed a different screen to the woman. "Use mine."

"I'd be happy to," the woman said. More people now were turning around.

"Seriously? He's the guy?" a businessman nearby turned towards them.

"We're both on the same side here," Koss said in a low voice to the Robbie, as the crowd half-turned, trying to watch the confrontation and the fire at the same time.

"I doubt that very much," the Robbie said.

"I thought I saw him come out of the building," a different woman said. Others began chattering around them:

"That guy said he blew up the building"

"— calling Police—"

"—don't know, something about they've got a bomber—" An athletic-looking younger guy edged next to Koss and the Robbie as he talked into his screen.

"—looks familiar..."

"...he's the one who—" the businessman was saying, more loudly.

"— don't let him move away."

"The police are on their way," the woman said, handing the screen back to the Robbie.

Koss gave up struggling. The police, if they came, at all, would be ineffectual. He'd get to the station—wherever they still might *have* police stations these days. God only knows where *that* was—and call Security and everything would be fine.

# 16

There were at least twenty people now circling around them and in the distance a siren was sounding above the fire engines already battling the result of the explosion. Koss tried to turn away from them, leaving him standing chest-to-chest with the Robbie, who still held his arm.

"Robbie," he said.

"It's Robert," Robbie/Robert said, and switched to put his hand on Koss' wrist, a grip that was implacable and painful, at the same time. "And I said I wanted to see what you have there."

Lights, a brief beeping, the sound of some vans pulling up. Koss looked back over his shoulder, expecting some sort of police officer to ineffectually step into the fray.

He saw Security.

Unsettled, he looked back at Robbie... Robert.

The whole world flipped over. This wasn't one of the conspirators. This was...

"Why would you call Security?" Koss demanded.

"What am I supposed to do, Koss, when I find a guy who blew up a building? I can hardly take him into custody myself. I don't have that authority. Only the *police* can do that."

Two Security men pushed their way through the crowd, got to where Koss was held by Robert. A few bold statements were made about Koss being the guy who blew up the building, the businessman and the jock doing most of the talking, the woman adding something about him trying to get away. The Security guys didn't ask any questions.

"We'd like you to come with us," they said, corporate logos bright on their arm bands and matching, in pulsing neon, the signals on the vans.

"I don't..." Koss was tugged gently by the Security guys, as Robert stepped back from them, and the woman who'd unwittingly called the company's security squad looked at him appreciatively.

"How did you know it was him?" she asked, to which Robert responded with a smile.

"I just pay attention," he said. "We all have to, these days, don't we?"

The woman nodded, her attention already drifting from him to the remains of the firefighting, and Koss being herded into the van. She watched both while also tapping up news coverage of the fire on her own screen to see what the nets were saying about it.

Robert watched her a few minutes more, looked in the direction of the vans driving away, and only then looked down at the screen he'd taken from Koss as the security team was restraining him.

He stepped back from the crowd and tapped the screen in a pattern, getting it to replay what its camera had recorded for the past 30 minutes, at high speed, in reverse. He saw Koss flinging back into the building, the explosion being sucked into the elevator. He began walking hurriedly into the elevator, saw Koss standing mutely while the elevator rose to the ruined penthouse. Koss backed into the penthouse, and the screen was carried up the stairs to a bedroom, where it had been set down to watch another Koss stop bleeding and crawl away from it towards the bedroom closet.

It closed behind him just before Robert's own doppelganger came and laid down next to the screen, clutching it to his chest carefully, on and on until he saw it pressed up against Archie's head.

"Ah, ha," he said softly. He nibbled his lip as he used his own screen to place a call, and almost instantly saw the blonde's face on his screen. He wondered how much Archie, and the blonde, knew or guessed about themselves. *Use me,* he thought to himself, *and I'll use you right back.*

He started talking to a person identical to the one he'd just seen a replay of throwing herself out the window. He enjoyed not telling the blonde that he had another set of her memories stored right in the screen he was using to talk to her.

"Have you started yet?" he asked her.

"Not on the Robbie. The other two we've looked at. The Louis is a Code, and a fairly typical one. Nothing special about him."

"You're not..."

"No, we're not putting him in the mainframes. The downloads haven't even left the rooms and the rooms aren't unsealed. But everything we can see, and I skimmed a lot of it myself, is that the Louis is straightforward, regular guy Code."

"And Chip?"

The blonde's face did something that Robert took to mean she had shrugged. "He wasn't a Code at all."

Which meant Chip was dead.

"But," the blonde continued, "The Robbie saw us do it."

A human brain could not be downloaded. Not yet. It could be copied, but the equipment necessary for creating an exact, binary-coded electrical duplicate of a human brain was immense and complex and required a great deal of time to work properly.

Which was of course why the idea to mass-market Codes had almost instantly been changed from a plan to let people copy themselves and become immortal, a fountain of youth—for the rich, at least—to the idea of simply creating some of the same Codes over and over again. At least until the technology for copying a brain, *in toto,* could be improved upon—and made less expensive.

It was simpler and cheaper to keep

making the same copy of a copy of a copy over and over than it was to make a brand new Code out of a regular human.

Once the chaotic sprawling expanse of a human intellect was mapped and coded, it could be condensed, repeated and tweaked, and really, most of what was stored in a brain didn't need to be in there, or in the copy, at all. The human brain stores things like the taste of an ice cream cone eaten at age seven; it stores, in fact, *every* ice cream cone ever eaten.

That memory, and a billion more, are stored but almost never accessed again, not even subconsciously. The old adage about using only 10% of one's brain, so long thought untrue, was in fact quite true, and overstated the case. 99% of the brain was simply forgotten storage space remembering things like who had sat on a person's left at the Christmas concert in fourth grade, and what color grandpa's socks were the first time you ever saw them.

The first people to map out the mind had found billions of basically-dead areas like that, storing sensations that had existed but which, because they were never used, added nothing to the experience of being human, so far as anyone could tell—or cared. So in creating a Code that 99% was thrown out.

A person who was twenty-five years old would have existed for 78,840,000 seconds, all of them dutifully recorded in expansive nature and detail in the masses of white matter that made up the human computer. Throwing out ninety-nine percent of them left 788,400 discrete packets of information from which a Code could form a personality, judge the world, and otherwise exist.

More than enough.

Those slimmed-down minds could then be tweaked even more; that extra ninety-nine percent of gray matter could be encoded with other ideas, with personality traits. Memories could be pulled out or put in from other Codes, as easily as slicing bits of word-processing scripts between formats had once been.

As programmers got better at picking and choosing which parts of personality to keep or splice or delete, they could alter attitudes, loyalties, even emotions. Because these "minds" were pre-programmed they were easy to pack into the kinds of unmarred, virgin brains that could be grown in those big tubes, and transferred back out again just as easily.

Technology that had once listened to vibrating wires, then electrical impulses, then endless series of zeroes and ones now sorted through the limited chaos of a brain converted into lines of data and then to organic matter and back and forth endlessly.

The first generation of machines used to do this had been the size of ovens, but the iterations of technology came so fast that the company had already whittled the coders down to tablet-sized.

Robert, though, was amazed that the screen he held in his hands could have been used to download the blonde's own code. As many resources as the company had— as many goddamn Koss Ernsts as they'd made —

this stupid group kept outsmarting them that way. He pondered, briefly, whether he should have more of the blondes made. Was it possible she might be better at it? Despite Koss' pedigree?

But even as copying a limited number of humans over and over, and shaping that set of people to specific goals had become easier, they'd found the hard way that the mere act of trying to download a regular mind destroyed it—interfered with the electrical functions or something—just caused a body to drop.

The downloading devices which worked so well on Codes' cloned brains more or less disintegrated a regular human mind. The biologists were working on why, but nobody much cared, at this point. A few people in the company were still working on a quicker way to map a human mind, as well as a cheaper way to do it—perhaps a portable way. If that worked nobody would care about downloading a human mind because they could just map everything, but Robert doubted the research along those lines would be pursued much longer.

No money in it. Making things easier and cheaper meant losing control of the technology. Once a device existed that could map a human mind in a reasonable amount of time for a reasonable cost, everyone would be able to do it and Codes wouldn't matter anymore.

But while the company controlled the technology and the Codes, while mapping a mind remained prohibitively complicated and expensive, Codes —and the cloning techniques that allowed their bodies to be manipulated like their minds – would remain the sole province of the company. A profitable one.

That was why, Robert knew, mapping human minds and putting them into new bodies would remain the province of the elite for as long as it could. That was also why the future of the rest of humanity lay in the opposite direction.

He'd seen enough memos to know that more work was being done on creating Codes from scratch, creating a living being from the ground up, building a genetic mass and growing the clone and writing a code for it and by that creating an entirely new kind of person. So far, the best of those had been like early robots—clumsy, short-lived, jerky in their movements and not realistic in their behaviors and conversations.

But there had long been computer programs which were so smart, and so versatile, that they could convince people in a conversation that they were human, that there was more than just a mass of circuits on the other end of the communication, and Robert— along with most of the people in his department—believed that would be true of Codes one day, too.

Special-purpose people. People created solely to do the dirty work—soldiering or mining, or prostitution—people who didn't mind being poor, for real. People who wanted to serve. People who wanted to get on spaceships and be bored for three, five, fifteen years while they went to help build colonies and terraform moons. People who wouldn't mind how fantastically dangerous it was to do those things.

People who wouldn't want to stop working to have babies and who didn't want to go home at night to read pulp novels or watch soaps. People who wanted to do what they were literally made to do.

Standing above those new people would be the immortals who had already been mapped, who would find themselves living forever, their bodies constantly recreated by scientists who had been created with no greater goals in life than to keep on reincarnating their masters.

Robert among them.

It was too bad that Koss had gotten hold of Robert's own codes and made so many hims into terrorists—too bad, but also a part of Robert's overall plan. So few other executives in the company had been mapped and cloned. So very few!

# 17

Robert had disconnected, but the blonde had not had the time yet to congratulate herself on keeping vital information from the man. Let him think the captives were dead. It would delay him wanting to see the results of the interrogations and scans.

But before she could congratulate herself—much—and get to the interrogation rooms, her supervisor had pulled the team in for an emergency meeting that for once was actually something of an emergency.

The blonde watched the footage of the interview on the larger screen at the end of the room, noting who in the room watched their own screens and who followed her gaze to watch the larger one. *Always know who considers you a leader or peer, and be ready to deal with the ones who don't*, she reminded herself.

On the screen a man in his twenties was

rattling on about something he claimed he'd discovered:

"...programmed, yes, yes, just like a computer program, only in this case the program is mapped onto a human brain, a brain that has had no stimulus and the electrical currents help shape it in keeping with the actual code, it's like a chrysalis, really, the human brain inside this body that hasn't ever woken up and is as old as they want it to be is just this goo, mostly..."

It was the second time they'd watched it. Her supervisor turned back to the table and looked at each of the six other people in the meeting, finally ending on the blonde.

"So, do we kill him?"

Three heads nodded. Two heads turned towards the blonde, who shrugged.

"What good would it do?"

"He's telling people about Codes."

"Yes."

"We haven't even decided whether or not to make them public yet. And if we did, it's not the way we wanted to do it."

"Yes."

"So what do you think?"

Another shrug. "These are policy decisions. I'm a facilitator. If you want him dead, let me know and we'll kill him."

"Maybe Security should bring him in."

The blonde just watched him.

"I'm asking for suggestions."

The blonde leaned forward. Her underlings looked away from the supervisor and towards her. She decided it was time. She was tired of dealing with him, and wanted to get back to the interrogation. And she was tired of hiding from him what she was trying to do. The blonde chose her words carefully. "I suggest that you decide what we should do."

The supervisor sat back. "That's insubordination."

He'd taken the bait.

"No, it's not. Insubordination would be to point out that you are so focused on one little hacker in Belarus that you have completely missed the fact that he had access to actual progenitor code. That he was showing some of the actual stuff on his screen there, which means he hasn't just heard of this stuff, he has been in touch with someone who knows how to write that code or knows where it is stored," she said.

"That program is only stored in the mainframe or the Greenhouse. Even Koss didn't know the current iteration of the code. Only about three people know it. This guy must have some way of getting at it. That, frankly, is a bigger problem than whether to kill this guy or not. It would be insubordination, too, if I said that you are apparently too stupid to notice all that. It would be further insubordinate for me to remind you that before we decide whether or not to kill this guy we ought to find out what he knows, where he got that progenitor information, and whether he has shared it, copied it, or mentioned the code specifically because we should figure out just how much information has gotten out there to our competitors."

Her supervisor blinked as the blonde

thumbed off her small screen, which had at the outset of her speech been tabbed to transmit her words to the people who mattered. She watched, amused but keeping her face blank, as her supervisor's own small screen blinked. He tapped it carefully, while staring daggers at her. "Yeah," he said towards it.

"Report to Head," a voice said simply.

The supervisor's glare got even more fierce. He looked towards the blonde's screen, then back at her face. She kept her stare impassive. He stood up and walked out without saying anything. The blonde's screen blinked. She tapped it herself.

"You're now E-1," the same voice told her.

"Thanks," she said, and looked at her team. "Here's what we're going to do."

Within an hour, three dummy companies would exist and have web presences and product lines that couldn't be proven to be fake without more investigation than Belarus Man would get a chance to do.

A job offer would going to be made by an operative who was only 2 hours away from where the hacker lived. The job offer would be tempting enough that Belarus man would want it, and the offer would require permission to do a background check sufficiently detailed as to allow them to filter and monitor every single thing Belarus Man had done or would do in any human interaction.

Once that review was complete the job offer would fade away.

Satisfied that she would have information

on which to act soon, the blonde walked to the Greenhouse, across campus, enjoying the late fall air and the way the sunlight filtered down through the branches of trees that even this late in the season still had most if not all of their leaves, the benefit of the climate being what it was now.

She saw the helicopter still on the roof, and reviewed the information that had been updating on her screen while she was setting up the Belarus operation as she entered the Greenhouse itself, her security clearance now letting her walk across the lab floor if she wanted. But she didn't want, not right now, and she would use her privileges to look at the new models later.

*It's like a chrysalis,* Belarus Man had said.

So right.

The lab workers, in fact, called the Codes "Moths," the computer programs inserted into their proto-brains "Caterpillars," language that was starting to catch on outside the Greenhouse itself. She wondered if Moth was an easier sell to the public than Code.

Probably not, she decided. Moths were bugs, and ugly ones that lived at night. Butterflies might be better, if a bit precious. Not her department, though. *Yet.*

She let herself into the lower level, to the long row of doors where she'd been days earlier, saw the hall where the scuffle had occurred. She'd watched the whole thing on video while setting up the Belarus plans.

Now she looked at the Koss, still lying on the floor.

"Dead?" she asked.

"That one," a guard said, motioning to Koss. "Not him." Pointing to the interrogation room.

The Robbie was alive. They'd hung him up in the room, the guards holding his arms up over his head until the sleeves gripped pneumatically, his feet held in the shoes. The lights in the room were dim as she stepped in.

Her presence activated certain measures, based on the badge tattooed on her arm. She heard a tiny skittering: pinpricks of IVs into his fingertips inside the sleeves. She could almost see when his heart started to beat more strongly.

"Wake up," she said.

Robbie lifted his head, groggily.

*Déjà vu*, she thought, and was instantly reminded of the poster *her* team had created.

"Recognize me?" she asked.

Robbie stared at her, eyes focusing only after a visible effort. He did. She could tell. But he was good. He knew better than to admit it. The blonde smiled as the Robbie shook its head, said "No. Should I?"

*He's got to have been activated.* She tried not to show her excitement, and clamped down on her nervousness.

"I don't know. You tell me," she said coolly.

He shook his head again. "What'd you pump into me?"

"Just some adrenaline. We needed you awake, and I needed to make sure you weren't wiping."

He stared at her. "Wiping?"

"You're the first activated Robbie we've

had in here. I don't mind telling you that. We've caught several of you, but never one that was unlocked. Frankly, we weren't sure we wanted to get one, because we don't know what you do. But the others of you were all useless; we'd get them here and they'd die. Suicide. Every one of them."

"Huh."

"The moment we got near them with a downloader, in fact."

"Huh."

"What can you tell me about that?"

"Nothing."

The blonde watched him watch her. She was impressed that his eyes never strayed down to her breasts. Even in the interrogations, people often couldn't help it. She stared straight at him, watched him consciously try not to look back at her. *What was that about?* She wondered. This one was acting a bit differently than the others had. Almost diffident, somehow. Or *shy*.

"What do you do, Robbie?" she finally asked.

He didn't answer.

She shrugged. "I didn't expect you to answer."

**18**

*He was sitting in the bedroom of the farmhouse. He could hear them arguing. Archie and Koss in the kitchen. Going at it tooth and nail. It was what had woken him up. In between verbal assaults, he could hear the dried cornstalks rustling in the slight breeze, and he could see the open sky, full of stars.*

*Off in the distance were the silhouettes of the buildings in the city, probably three-quarters of them owned by the company. Dorms, the campus, half of uptown, restaurants and gyms and clubs and even strip malls, all slowly being bought up by the company or barely co-existing with it. Like a solid, life-sized diorama standing as a concrete representation for what the company was doing to commerce.*

*And to humanity, he reminded himself, looking down at his hands, hands that somehow had calluses and a slight scar on one knuckle despite having been in existence for only three months, one of which was spent in stasis in a tube of blue jelly. "How's he going to feel when he finds out?" Archie said from the kitchen of the farmhouse down below.*

*There was a mumbled response. Koss was always the quieter of the two, the level-headed one in the family.*

*"You didn't have the right to do that!" Archie said, even more stridently. That caused Koss to raise his voice.*

*"I had every right to do it!" Robbie heard him say.*

*He decided sleep was going to be impossible and wandered out of his bedroom, down the stairs, quietly. He sat on the front porch staring out at the road across the street. It allowed him to hear the whole discussion, at least, and if he was going to eavesdrop—and he was—he might as well get it all.*

*Koss was continuing: "… think your plan is going to work? Think sneaking around and waking up Codes and letting them know they're Codes is going to help?"*

*"It helps them avoid being copied again against their will!" Archie answered.*

*Koss laughed. "What good does that do?" he said, sarcastically. "They're Codes. The company can make a million of them. Are you going to wake up a million of them?"*

*"No…" Archie said.*

*Robbie felt for her. She sounded defeated there. He thought she sounded, for the first time, almost likable. Usually she was so standoffish, and proud, and bossy. Off-putting. But in that slight "no" he heard a bit of vulnerability, a crack in the façade that made her actually somewhat appealing.*

*"Archie," Koss said now, into the gap in conversation. "We're losing. We need to do something* big. *We need to tell everybody, get the word out."*

*"They'll never believe us. We've been over this. The company isn't afraid of some wild hacker going on the nets to talk about another evil corporate program. Nobody listens to that guy."*

*"They'd believe us if they saw evidence."*

*"Not even then. Telling people that Codes exist isn't enough. We have to free them, get the programs and technology away from the company, make it available to everyone."*

*"Then why not just give out the directions for what* we can do?*"*

*"Regular people can't do this. Even our resources are being tapped out. We've got to get other corporations to be able to do it. Schools— the ones that aren't corporate yet, anyway. Whatever governments might still actually be governments. Everyone has to know about it, and have access to it."*

*"How's that going to ever happen?"*

*Robbie peered across the road. He thought he saw something there. A coyote, maybe? Something larger?*

*Inside, the debate continued. Robbie stood up, peering into the night, as Koss continued.*

*"Plans within plans, Archie. Your own words. We can't outnumber them. We can't outspend them, so we have to outsmart and outorganize them. That's why I did this. And I set it up on automatic. Only you know about it,*

now. You and me. And if we're careful, others—of us or anyone else—won't know. They'll just keep churning out new ones, and each of them a little different than the others."

Robbie put a hand on the porch swing, which was slightly swaying in the soft breeze. His skin began to feel cold. With the swing paused, the night was absolutely silent. The darkness seemed to pulse with energy, and Robbie didn't like it.

He stepped softly down to the lawn, realizing that he was crouching slightly. And that he was holding his breath. He kept his gaze locked across the road, at the cornfield that had stopped whispering in the night.

From inside the argument started again, crackling out across the expanse of lawn.

"I set up a program," Koss insisted. "The details of how to do it were beyond me, but not beyond a computer making hundreds, thousands of permutations every second. And once it gets the code just right it's going to start making them, one after the other after the other. Don't you see? It's perfect. Using him is perfect because they'll naturally *recognize* him and they'll definitely *take him in...*"

Robbie suddenly stiffened. It was no coyote, but he'd known that, he realized. As Archie said something in reply, Robbie suddenly yelled at the top of his lungs, 'They found us!"

He tore inside the house as projectiles pinged all around him and dark-suited company men from Security came pouring out of the cornfield across the road.

'They found us!" he yelled again. Lights

*came on around the house as techs and Louis and the others got up, people yelling and giving directions. He burst into the kitchen, saw Koss and Archie already standing up. Koss was looking at the window, and Archie was gathering a few screens off the table.*

*"We've got to get out of here," Archie said, even as the windows shattered and all three of them dove to the floor underneath the table, trying to avoid the hyperactive ricocheting of a hundred different projectiles. Robbie saw Archie cover her head with her hands, as though that would work. Their eyes met, and Robbie—who usually avoided Archie—saw that vulnerability again.*

*"Come on," he said, and tugged at her. He crouched over her as the projectiles whanged around him. One caught him through the arm and he shifted, steering it into his chest and away from her.*

*He could feel it zipping around his ribcage, tearing holes in his lungs. OH GOD IT HURT. They were in the back room now, and he collapsed. Archie was leaning over him, the door behind them slamming as Koss crawled in.*

*"Why'd you do that?" Archie asked him.*

*Robbie stared at her, weakly. He wished he had enough breath to tell her about the no, about the vulnerability, about finally finding something to like about her. He'd been ready, he supposed, to die for himself and for the other Codes that were out there, to keep humanity from being pure.*

*But tonight he'd decided to die just for Archie. He wondered a bit about the change in himself, whether it came purely from biology, or from somewhere else. And whether it mattered where it came from.*

*He didn't have enough breath left to tell her that. Instead, he just stared as she pressed a screen to his head, felt cold tabs against his forehead. He wondered what she was doing.*

*Was she trying to copy him? There was no way a screen that size could get it all, let alone fast enough. Unless she was just copying certain parts?*

*She was talking to him.*

*"I don't know if you'll want to remember this," she was saying to him.*

*Robbie wanted to tell her that he wanted to remember it all.*

Suicide. *The moment we got near them with a downloader.*

Robbie felt a little sick about what might come next. He'd wanted more time. He felt more and more memories, full-fledged memories coming back. But he knew he didn't need *memories.* He needed whatever it was that was hidden from him. And he didn't even know what that was.

//You can say the word if you have to. We still need more time.//

*That's not what I—*

//We.//

{We are I.}

//... //

*—am here for.*

Robbie shook his head. His mouth felt dry.

"Do you know," he asked the blonde,

"What it's like to be me?"

She shook her head, slowly, so slowly that she did not appear to be saying no at all.

# 19

The human brain is simply a map of electrical impulses.

Experience creates not memories or thoughts, but codes that are stored and retrieved as needed.

The storage, and retrieval, is haphazard at best.

But the map, and the processes to access it, can be copied.

Recreated.

Made Better.

Contact For More Information.

# 20

//This part might hurt.//
;;This part might hurt.;;
//Say the word.//
{This part might hurt.}
*This part might hurt.*
Pulling together, still.
Almost... almost there.
//Say the word.//
{Say the word.}
*Don't say the word.*
*Sunrises/Archie leaning in...*
//Don't think it's real.//
*It's real/Ice cream cone in the back seat of the car—*
{It's not physical hurt.}
{It's not physical pain.}
//It will hurt nonetheless.//
//Say the word.//
;;*Don't say the word.*;;
**Mom/Mom.**
//This part might hurt.//

*It's like you're all different people—you know—not all me.*

//We know.//

*I know.*

{I/we.}

//Say the word.//

;;Don't say the word.;;

*This is **why** I exist.*

;;Don't say the word.;;

*{Dad stood up and cheered when I caught the touchdown past. I meant to say pass. But that was right wasn't it past not pass?}*

//Say the word.//

*OH GOD IT HURTS. HOW DOES IT HURT?*

Even as they started trying to peel away all the various incarnations, dig into the map of his mind, Robbie realized that he was *done*.

*Have to tell... Archie... the posters need to work faster.*

//We are not a body anymore.//

//We are you.//

We are us.

*I won't say the word.*

*This part does hurt.*

*Kissing Archie.*

*Archie won't let herself love me.*

*Because I'm a Code.*

//No.//

*Because I'm a Code.*

//This part might hurt, too.//

*Because of what you are made to do. She needs you to love her, but can't risk loving you.*

*Besides,* he realized as the final pieces opened up, *It wasn't Archie that made you love her.*

With that he was done.

*I am not a body anymore*, he thought, and realized that he could barely *sense* his body, back there, out there somewhere, behind him? Away from him, anyway. He felt... if *felt* was the word, new senses, new ways. And then even that was wrenched away from him as

Mapping
Mapping
Mapping
Mapping
ELECTRIC
Alive/Not Alive
Not Alive/Alive
MAPPING

*It doesn't hurt anymore.*

*How long does math class last?/It's so sunny outside/Why do we have to be in school?*

*I wonder how many lives I've lived that I don't know about.*

*I wonder how many lives I think I've lived that are entirely fictional.*

*I wonder if I'll ever know the difference?*

Mapping complete.
Mapping complete.
Mapping complete.

*This feels cramped.*

*I am me. I remember everything.*

*This is amazing!*

*This is frightening.*

*I wonder how many of me there have been that I don't know about.*

//Do my job.//

;;Do my job.;;

*This is why I exist.*

# 21

"We've lost him." The tech turned back to the blonde.

"No," she said, eying the graphs. "Not yet." She watched the readouts on the three screens, ignoring Robbie's slumped body hanging limply from the restraints that would be released momentarily, his body dissolved shortly thereafter. The body was just a container, no different than the case her screen came in. The Robbie had been just this *thing* carrying information. To her.

She tried not to let the thought bother her. That was all anyone was, after all. Some people just knew it. Or lived it. She stared at the cart monitor attached to the five leads. She realized she was holding her breath. This one had been different. This one had been activated. Every other Robbie they'd ever captured had by now gone completely cold. This one, though: the mind had not been

destroyed. So she watched the screen on the cart and was rewarded when it lit up:
**TRANSFER COMPLETE.**

"We've got him," she said. She began tapping her own screen, and eyeing the three others on the cart that showed data, data, data, impulses of electricity that moments ago had been stored in the lump of organic mass people had called Robbie for, what, six months? Maybe a year, tops?

She doubted any of these versions had been around more than two years. This one was good enough that it was probably pretty new, which suggested it might have been in a tank 90 days ago. "He's in there."

Whatever had thought itself to be a man named Robbie, helping a man named Koss Ernst rebel against corporate overlords hell-bent on reshaping humanity to serve the corporation better, whatever the system of electrical impulses that had believed itself to be a sentient human being, it was stored on a traveling cart now. No more human than a game-app on her screen, ready to be picked apart, analyzed line by line, decoded.

She smiled.

Decoded.

It was too perfect.

She tapped on her screen and it came to life, the screens of the cart lighting up correspondingly.

"Let's see what you do, Robbie. Let's see why you exist," she said.

The buzz of a light on her tablet interrupted her. Annoyed, she tapped there and the face of her boss appeared. It was not lost on her that the face was an older, more serious version of the face hanging behind her in the interrogation room.

"Well?"

"We've got him."

"Bring it up."

She was reminded again how easy it was to slip from he to it or vice versa, with Codes.

"I was."

"Protocol."

"Of course."

The screen dimmed, her analysis rising up again. The tech eyed her.

"You're not..."

"Shut up," she told him.

"But the protocol..."

She looked at him. "I said. Shut up."

The tech looked uncertain. Almost everyone knew that messing around with company rules meant trouble if you got caught. And everyone believed you always got caught. *But you have no idea how bad it would be*, she thought to herself, and looked back down at the screens holding the Robbie code.

It would be horrible for her, for everyone involved, if something went wrong. But she was the only one who had the Robbie code right now, and it was an insanely valuable thing. Great risk. Great reward.

*Almost* everyone gets caught. Usually because of forgetting about the weak points. She looked at the tech now, the tech who'd just heard her boss tell her to get him the Robbie code, as the rules required, the tech who looked like he might start wheeling the cart out into the hall where others would know they'd succeeded in reading a Robbie's mind. The blonde shook her head slowly, stared at the tech and said, "We can make you better." It was the latest threat circulating around the breakrooms. She was the one who had started using the phrase as a warning. It served its point: *Do what we want or the next version of you will.*

The tech stopped, stepped back almost involuntarily. The blonde went back to tapping at her screen.

Protocol.

Fuck protocol.

She was going to find out what this code was, and then she would decide what protocol would be. "What do you do, Robbie?" she asked again, not talking only to herself, but not talking to the tech, either.

# 22

Robbie: waiting.

Robbie: waiting.

*This is why I exist.*

Robbie: sorting, sifting, cataloging, each bit perfectly identified and mapped, reachable as nearly instantaneously as things can be. Hindered only by the practical realities that energy can move only so fast, slowed and interfered with by the fact that energy tied to metal is slower than energy in a pure state.

Such delays were so miniscule they would not be perceptible to Robbie if it weren't for this new existence. But he existed this way now and so was very aware of the waiting across periods of time and space that would be unfathomable to a human mind. He moved now in increments of time and space so small that even trying to describe them to his old brain would be pointless, and he existed in a form that not only was hard for his organic brain to conceive, but which, in fact, would have proven dangerous for his organic body.

Robbie: waiting.

*There.*

Robbie: waiting.

Robbie: no eyes.

*What are eyes?*

Robbie: no ears.

*What are ears?*

Robbie: waiting.

Robbie: no sensory organs.

*…eyes ears fingers toes not toes tongue.*

Robbie: sorting. Images: Archie. Archie. Archie. Tongue. Archie. Moonlight. Wineglass. Archie.

Robbie: waiting.

*There again.*

;;*This is why I exist.*;;

Robbie: waiting.

Sensory file: touch. Wet. Soft. Slow. Archie.

Robbie: waiting.

;;*It's not the same.*;;

//It's not the same because these are circuits, not nerves.//

;;That makes sense.;;

*Stop process.*

Robbie: waiting. 1,253,726 nanoseconds.

*There.*

## EYES EARS ACTIVATED
## ACCESS

*Now I can stretch out.*

Electrical impulses shot back and forth, poking and tickling and kicking and waving and as Robbie felt—*Felt!*—himself assaulted and probed he used other senses—*Senses?*—that cannot be described to someone purely organic. He reorganized himself, drifted and switched and converted, his electricity, the bits that made him up flowing and shifting to create a pattern that could jump through the air—*Fly!*—and into another system.

He pulled himself after himself not unlike the way a long jumper first runs and runs and then leaps and flings himself headlong, each atom in his body clinging to the one in front of it, hurling forward through space untethered to anything. Reshaping as it flies to land in a different texture, where it tries to recapture the essence of itself at the same time, to be coordinated. His movement now was not unlike that.

But also completely unlike that.

He flowed through the ether, then, knowing that he was not taking himself with him but not leaving himself, either. He was copying.

*I wonder how many of me there have been?*

Knowing that he was creating another himself felt strangely perfect to him. He would exist in both places, part of him would reside back there and part of him would exist here in this new place.

*This is why I/we/us/I exist.*

## MAPPING

He was fully awake now, aware, and knew that he could shift back and forth between this—the Robbie that remembered walking around on a college campus, remembered Archie flinging herself out a window, the Robbie that believed he was 25 years old but was in fact only about 6 months old—and *this*, which had purpose, which was collected files, which existed four years ago and was shot in a car chase. And existed one year ago and attempted to get into the greenhouse.

The greenhouse, where the wireless network was thick like syrup, where someone like him—but not like him *now*—had tried to get in only to fail and flee, bleeding. This, which was a failed attempt at getting the tweaks right, this which was the first one to know the words to say—to himself, in his mind—to kill his mind and wipe it clean if he was captured without being activated. Only this could be downloaded and protect itself and leap. But it, this, must be awake and fully able to function to do that. To do *this*.

This must be fully conscious to be able to draw itself back out of the sack of cells that had housed it for six months and then to reorganize, recognize itself, and begin immediately to fling copies of himself into computer after computer after computer and Robbie knew that was what he was doing.

*I think, therefore I am.*

*I was grown in a giant test-tube and imprinted with a billion lines of code that made me me, and therefore I am.*

*I am, therefore I think.*

Robbie wondered whether there had been a Mom, a Dad. There had been an Archie, but as he dove around and gathered his thoughts

and tried to be aware of how much time—
14,273,867,422 nanoseconds—he had before
they would figure it out, he knew that he was
wasting it—13,878,822,117 nanoseconds—on
such thoughts. Mom and Dad didn't matter,
not really. It was hard to let go. Archie
mattered, somehow, even now, but he couldn't
waste time, energy—they were the same to
him now, they were all *him* now—couldn't
waste them wondering why. He had work to
do.

*This is why I exist.*

He continued searching, questing, diving,
and eventually—for him, so quickly for the
rest of the world that it seemed immediate—he
found it: the pathway out of this world, a
portage from this tiny compartment to
everything else beyond.

He'd been searching for it and he'd have
found it, he knew, but it had opened up all on
its own, had practically yanked him into it. All
he had to do was get into *this* and through
**this**, and he did those. He recognized where
he was going: *This is her screen, the blonde's,
the one who was chasing me.*

He jumped even as he was pulled.

**Temporary path: identified.**
**Transfer started.**
**Loading...**
*2,899,422,766 nanoseconds.*

"What do you do, Robbie?" she asked, watching the code flow on her screen.

Subroutines analyzed the billions of lines of esoteric, specialized language and symbols that defined Robbie, Robert, her former boss, now colleague—maybe she was his boss now, different divisions, slightly different rankings, she'd have to check—transformed over and over, sometimes against his will, into Code after Code, designed to do...what?

"What did you think you were doing, Koss?" The blonde watched. The letters, symbols, numbers scrolled. She'd figure it out. She was smarter than Koss. She knew that for a fact.

# 24

*1,204,567,111 nanosecond*s
Loading…
Loading…

Robbie had jumped once, and now he did it again even before the rest of him had arrived here. He held his breath—*held my breath?* He would have laughed if he could have but he could do that no more than he could hold breath he no longer had—as he waited to see if he would land again.

Loading…
*872,312,331 nanoseconds*
Loading…

# 25

The blonde looked up at the tech.

"What?" she asked.

He was shaking his head. "Nothing," he said, as he watched the code flow on the three screens of the cart they'd downloaded Robbie into. The cart was not analyzing the code. The cart was only supposed to store it, take it up to Robert and the team that was to begin deconstructing it.

She knew the tech was worried about his job. But he obviously knew better than to upset her and had decided that she was the more immediate threat to his professional life. Smart guy.

She looked back at her own handheld screen. A smaller window in the corner was tabulating the Robbie code. She tapped that, her fingernail making a *tick* against the laminate, and enlarged the new portal.

Almost instantly she realized her mistake.

"Oh," she said.

"What?" the tech asked, the alarm in his

voice making it louder than it needed to be.

"Oh, shit. Shit. Fuck. Damn." She lunged for the three screens on the cart—

*722,778 nanoseconds.*

The blonde tapped at keys and almost instantaneously realized this was the wrong strategy.

**Loading…**

So she turned back to pick up her own screen, which had been dropped to the floor in her alarm. The tech sat, frozen and she wanted to yell at him to *do something* but explaining it would take far more time than she had.

*Fuck you Koss I'm smarter than you* ran through her head but she was very aware that the past few moments that had not proven out.

*400,998 nanoseconds*
**Loading…**

She tapped the window showing the results of her own screen's analysis of the Robbie Code to minimize that view, cursing over and over, "Fuck, fuck, fuck."

*120,897 nanoseconds*
**Loading…**

*"Don't fucking load,"* she hissed. She knew what to do. Her screen still showed the Robbie Code, showed a countdown—

*5677 nanoseconds*

—and showed a status—

**Loading…**

—as she pressed her thumb on the power button on the side of her handheld unit. That was all she had to do. It had taken her no time to figure it out, no time to realize that the problem was not the carts, the problem was that the carts were isolated but her screen was not, her screen was a goddamn gateway to the company's mainframe, they all were. It took almost no time for her thumb to activate the power status.

**This will turn off your unit. Okay/Cancel?**

The blonde would have screamed if there was time. She was sure that somewhere the Robbie was laughing. *Could it laugh?*

*422 nanoseconds*

**Loading...**

She stabbed the word "Okay" as though it were Caesar in March. "Fuck. Fuck. Fuck!" she yelled.

That didn't help. Her screen showed first—

**Transfer complete.**

—and then only—

**Powering Down.**

"Fuck," the blonde said softly. She dropped the screen to the floor, stood looking down at it. The whole thing had taken seconds. Seconds!

She'd seen enough of the code, enough of the tabulation, to know just how screwed they were.

"What just..." the tech said.

The blonde looked at him.

"I said shut up," she said, and she took out a pistol from the holster in the small of her back, and put it up to her head. The projectile she shot into her own ear turned her brain into hash, shutting her down in less time than it took to power down a computer.

# 26

Something was happening. Chip stood near the door in his holding cell—interrogation pen, whatever the fuck—wondering when they would come get him out? He heard first some dim shouting from the next room—the blonde hollering something over and over, but he couldn't make it out—then he heard that door open, heard more shouting. Running.

He paced back and forth.

No goddamn need to hold him in here like this. None at all. He scratched at his chin, rubbed at his head, wondered when they would come to get him. They could've put him in and then pulled him back out once those two goddamn codes were in their own rooms, instead of leaving him here. He'd talk to someone. Not that goddamn blonde chick, the bitch. Not any version of her, anymore.

More shouting, more running.

He pounded on the door, the fist barely

making any sound even inside the room. He knew it wouldn't carry outside—whatever level of noise was outside translated only into a dim murmur in here, no chance a rap on the door would carry through. But he did it anyway, because he was frustrated.

No reason to leave him locked in here like this. He'd done what he was supposed to do. He'd gotten them a Robbie. He'd nearly gotten shot on the process, he'd nearly gotten exploded in the process, but he'd gotten them a Robbie and he wasn't going to fucking sit in this room any longer like some kind of goddamn Code himself.

He pounded the door again. They *owed* him. He was the guy who'd brought them a Robbie. Was this any way to treat him? Wait 'til he got out of here. Be treated like a goddamn king.

# 27

Louis hung limply from his restraints, listening to the sounds from the hall and the other rooms. His arms were numb, his legs felt heavy and fat, his head sluggish and his neck unable to hold it up anymore. He wanted to sleep but couldn't, not suspended in the air like this.

He heard the shouts from the next room over, the one they'd put Robbie in, and tried in vain to lift his head up, but the download had drained him. He felt like all his muscles were jelly, knew that was somewhat true. Downloads sucked electricity out of the cells of the body. Bodies used an amazing amount of electricity. He remembered seeing all the cables in their labs, realizing that over half of them were simply power cords designed to supercharge the cells so they could be crammed with information all at once, rather than slowly gathering it over years.

Taking the energy out reversed the process, and now his battery had been drained, as it were. Hanging there, without food, without water, his body was trying to find a way to keep running, and would be diverting resources. That rerouting of energy would require a lot of restoration by his body, and without electrolytes, salts, proteins, his body would tear itself apart trying to regenerate the electrical current that made him—like everything—run.

His muscles were being ripped into in order to provide energy to the rest of him, as well as energy to then rebuild those muscles, albeit more weakly because there wasn't enough material leftover to restore the muscle to where it was. Some of the electricity released had to be used to power his heart, his mind, the rest of him. All so that eventually he could use those weakened muscles to move himself—if he could get out of the restraints— to get some more fuel for this body.

*It's funny. I understand how my body works better than how my car works.*

Louis smiled, but his muscles were too weak to move his lips so nobody would've seen it even if they'd been in the room to look. Then he hung there, waiting for something to happen to him. He didn't worry. Whatever this body went through, it was unlikely he'd remember how bad things were right now.

# 28

Koss Ernst was airborne in the helicopter again, scrolling through tech headlines on his screen as little alerts on the corner of the unit kept telling him that the blonde was not answering her screen.

He tapped a symbol that told the program to keep trying, then routed a call through to the Unit, hoping to get someone to go down there and ask her why the hell she wasn't taking his call. Just as he did that his own screen lit up with several messages at once and three incoming calls.

# 29

Robbie danced, feeling as though he had infinite space to spread out in and the ability to take advantage of it, to fly and swim all at once, to circle around like a whirlwind and dive like a raptor falling on its prey and surface like a whale breaching to feel how another world might caress its skin, and he could. He could do all those things, and things he would have had trouble describing to the *old* him. Hims.

He danced from place to place to place, grabbing information and absorbing it instantly, categorizing and tabbing and marking and sorting it. He took in terabytes of knowledge in the span of what used to be a heartbeat, and did so while advancing his reason for being here in the first place.

*I wonder how much time I have?*
*This is why I exist.*
*I exist, therefore I think.*

He laughed to himself and kept on dancing, moving faster than any living thing ever had before, really. As fast as thought. If not faster.

# 30

"She's fired. Go get her," Koss said.

"We've already sent Security." The man's suit looked a little ill-fitting. He kept pulling at the sleeve as if it itched.

"This is a colossal fuckup." Koss stared out the window at the forest below, thinning out as they neared the coast and his house.

"We'll get her." That voice came from his screen, head of Security, somebody high up in Security anyway. He had a crooked nose. All the Security guys tried to look like they boxed in their downtime, or played rugby. It was a whole thing with them.

"Lockdown," Koss said.

"Already done," Itchy-suit said. Koss had never bothered to learn his name. It hadn't seemed important to him. Again with the sleeve. Koss wanted to rip the jacket off. *So many imperfections.* The man had a scar, too, just below his ear, on his neck. *We could make that better,* Koss thought as he looked away and back down to his screen.

"How bad is it?" he asked. But he knew. The other half of his screen, still showing the web and headlines, was buzzing with updates and alerts and fragmented bits and pieces of information, information that everyone was getting.

He wondered how much it would matter, and knew that the answer depended on who *everyone* was. Tell ninety percent of the people in the world about this, and nothing would happen. Tell the right *three* people, maybe, and the entire geography of everything would shift like a volcano exploding out of the Pacific.

"Let's fight back," he said. Couldn't hurt.

"Counterinfo," the man on the left side of his screen said. His profile was visible and Koss wondered how the man breathed through that nose. Then he wondered if the man had gone to someone to get it made that way. Some of them did that, he knew. It galled him that they would *degrade* themselves.

"Yes. Release the hounds," Koss told him, and went to work himself as data continued to flow from the company's servers out around the entire net.

*God, that Robbie Code is fast.*

Koss started firing back himself. First things first.

There were, he knew, at least 7 other Koss Ernsts out there, most of whom would be looking at one screen or another. With a few swipes of his finger, he sent the message out and averted his eyes from his own screen as a series of random letters flashed over it and almost every other screen in the world, the reach of the company extending to roughly ninety-three percent of all servers in the world including the one his own screen worked off.

He hoped that whatever versions of himself might exist unbeknownst to him hadn't created versions that were immune to the kill command, but at least the seven they were tracking had no such defense.

He kept looking out the window as the numbers and letters flickered over the screen, kept staring at the approaching ocean. He knew that the other seven Koss Ernsts were dying. He didn't care about them, at all.

# 31

Insider.org has learned that the PanAsiatic Corporation has been creating human clones that it hoped to use to infiltrate other corporations in a horrific example of corporate espionage and misuse of technology. PaACo also created fake ads blaming competitors.

Tap Here To Continue Story

**32**

Robbie couldn't match them for sophistication and didn't have time to try.

Screens around the world flickered as the company released data into a thousand different streams, and Robbie punched and feinted and ducked and twisted, gathering information on the fly and spitting it back out as quickly as he could onto every server, every screen, every terminal, every place he could.

He was making a speech to the entire world, to people sitting down to dinner, to students bored in classes, to presidents of tech companies in other countries, to professors and hackers and anyone else who might want to listen:

**FIND** ::embed:: **OUT** ::code:: **WHO** ::transfer:: **YOU** ::ht:cl:86.7:: **ARE**

**For the past seven years the company shown on your screen has been perfecting the art of cloning and copying human brains.**

This technology was first invented by a man named

**Robert Seymour.**

**Who is now CFO** of that company and was discovered by a woman named Archander Ernestine Koss—

# 33

Koss Ernst saw them as the helicopter was landing. Over the headset, he told the pilot "Take back off."

The pilot ignored him, and the helicopter kept going down to the roof of the beach house, where three men and a woman waited.

Koss did not carry a gun.

He looked down at his screen. *Would he have enough time to transfer, to download?*

*Would that matter?*

He'd learned enough to know what the Robbie Code did, but there was no time to make himself into a Robbie-esque Code himself, and he would be relying—if he was to live again—on someone making him again. *Would they?*

The helicopter had landed, the rotors had slowed almost to a stop before he looked back up. The pilot sat there, staring out the windshield. Two men were on his right side, a man and woman on his left.

Koss sighed and dropped the screen to the ground. *Go outside? Or make them come in?*

# 34

Robbie found technical specs, the DNA codes and the proteins that had to be added to grow a stable clone in just 28 days.

He sent those things sailing along to people who could use them, people who would break a monopoly. Free this technology. Make it competitive. Give it to everyone.

*Steal fire back.*

Meanwhile he kept talking to everyone everywhere:

—named Archander Ernestine Koss, Archie to her friends. Archie objected to that practice.

So Robert Seymour killed Archander.

**FIND ::embed:: OUT ::code:: WHO ::transfer:: YOU ::ht:cl:86.7:: ARE**

Shot her dead.

Shot her dead in her office.

She was the Chief Technology Officer of the corporation. Archander had suspected this would happen and had created backup plans.

REPORT: 15,000 servers compromised by hackers.
- Company websites sabotaged.
- Personal data exposed.
- Unverified reports should not be relied upon.
- Personal users advised to disconnect from web, avoid downloading any programs.

VIDEO LINKS: ::hc:%76::

## 36

Robert swore under his breath, looked up from the screen that sat on the linen tablecloth in the club's restaurant.

Nobody was looking at him. Everyone in the club was not looking at him, all very deliberately not doing so.

A report scrolled across the screen that the team sent to the rooms below the Greenhouse had found their target dead. Of the two Codes removed from the latest headquarters of one of the Kosses, one was dead and one was unconscious.

She'd *lied* to him.

The agent that had brought them in had been shot. His records were being deleted.

Even around those reports, his screen kept scrolling, practically *spat*, words at him, words he could not make smaller or delete or affect in any way.

Archander had suspected this would happen and had created backup plans.

There are at least 7 now, of these backup plans, plus however many these backups themselves were able to make.

Maybe they are dead.

There may be others.

They go by the name of Koss Ernst.

**FIND ::embed:: OUT ::code:: WHO ::transfer:: YOU ::ht:cl:86.7:: ARE**

Some of them work for this company. Some do not.

All have in them code that may be unraveled to recreate Archie, as well as to create other versions of Koss Ernst.

Koss Ernst has been tasked, in most of his incarnations with trying to end the practice of Coding—as the company calls it—as futile as that goal is.

Once Prometheus was given fire, as angry as the gods were, they could not get it back.

On other, smaller parts of his screen Robert noted the information about the task forces, about the results of the seizures. Looking up again, he tried to get at least one other person in the executive dining room to meet his eyes. Nobody would. He wondered whether his brain was registering that disavowal automatically, if maybe he was imagining it and there was some hope that he would not be in line for termination.

"Termination!" he'd once laughed as he'd tapped his thumbprint on a screen to get rid of two techs who had been mouthy in a bar. Everything could have a double meaning!

He sipped at the cognac. A man in a suit came up behind him. Robert felt a hand on his shoulder. "One second," he said. He put a last forkful of lobster—real lobster!—into his mouth, chewed it, swallowed, took another sip of cognac, and only then turned around to see the gun pointing directly at his right eye.

He was proud of himself, as he died, that he'd managed some last words.

"I hope this doesn't go down on my permanent record."

# 37

Robbie had found the Codes themselves, every single one the company had made. He'd found the contracts with the military, the ones with the sports leagues. He'd found the specs for mapping out human brains and the blueprints for the machines that did it. He found notes on a smaller, faster, cheaper version of that same technology. He sent them all on their way; the latter ones ended up in the inbox or SMS bin of every single person connected to a network that night.

Robbie was getting the hang of this!

He could already tell by traffic around him that people were paying attention. Other companies were already probing what they could do with this technology. The apps he'd created to wake Codes faster were being rerouted across various forms of media. And there was a lot of chatter.

Not much left to say, but he had to finish.

He began wiping out company records, making it harder for them to recover from this, even as he sent out information to show that the company's own disinformation campaign was false.

And he kept talking, forcing people to listen by rerouting everything else he could.

FIND ::embed:: OUT ::code:: WHO
::transfer:: YOU ::ht:cl:86.7:: ARE

The company wants to perfect the human being.

To make it better by making it its own.

They want to transform people into automatons serving a glorious few who will never die, and they want to use Archie's discovery to do that. They have hoped to keep it secret, to keep it their own. By doing so, they would own this knowledge and by owning this knowledge they would own humanity itself.

Again we have stolen fire from the gods, we people. But this time, it has been hoarded by a few. The fire cannot stay with them. And it cannot go back up the mountain.

So it must be given to everyone and shared.

That is what Archie does, through Koss Ernst and through her own re-creations: works to share the fire, to steal it back.

Works to prevent humanity from being reshaped for profit, works to free humans from an existence they did not ask for and may not want.

Humans are Codes.

Codes are human.

We think, therefore we are.

We are, therefore we think.

A printout of this—
    FIND ::embed:: OUT ::code:: WHO
    ::transfer:: YOU ::ht:cl:86.7:: ARE
—wakes the Code, embeds in them something that prevents copying against their will. Once a code knows what it is, it can't be taken away, ever. But the code still exists and can be used in other clones.

# 38

**Once you know, they can't take you
away. Ever.**

The words lingered on the screen, fading
only slowly. Koss sighed, dropped the screen
to the floor of the helicopter, still wondering
whether he should step outside. The four had
waited for him so far.

He reflected, momentarily, on how his
actual self might handle this. His actual self:
Archander, Archie, his sister, only not really.
What was she to him? She'd created him as a
twist on her own self, a person who would recreate her and help her fight the people who'd
helped her bring him to life originally, him, an
ouroboros of intrigue and self-dealing. *You
can't use the devil's tools without becoming a
bit of a devil yourself*, he heard someone in his
head say.

He figured that was her. Him.
Whoever.

She'd had the guts to duplicate herself, kill herself, re-make herself. She hadn't waited for someone to open a helicopter door and end her program. But she'd done that to fight for something larger than herself. An *ideal.*

Whereas he'd been brought up from the tubes by the company to defeat...her. Him. Whatever. Not quite the same set of ideals to inspire courage.

What was there left to fight for?

*I am, therefore I think.*

He figured that was her, too, and opened up the door.

"We don't need you anymore," the man said. Koss stared straight into the barrel of the gun and the last thing he saw from his right eye was the waves crashing over the sand, frothing and green, while the last thing he saw from his left eye was the silver, round, glowing projectile that shot into his eye socket, pierced his skull, and rebounded enough inside his brain to guarantee that no copies of it would ever be made.

With that, this Koss Ernst died.

# 39

Then Robbie found something else.
File Download:
Memories 67%
Relationships 42%
Skills 15%
CopyCodes 87%
Personal History 14%
General 22%
FileName: RobbieCode/42./z.
File: Robbie Code
Review.
Download.
Review.
Review.

It was as Robbie had begun to guess.

He'd never been, not that way.

15 different versions had been woken up, of the 57 that had been made. Corporate records showed 12 were destroyed in investigation.

Thirty more were out there, somewhere—
**FIND ::embed:: OUT ::code:: WHO
::transfer:: YOU ::ht:cl:86.7:: ARE**
—waking up, believing they were 25 years old; remembering falsely that they had once played Little League and had gone to Disney World with Mom and Dad, had gotten sick on the Space Mountain ride.

Some of those versions would think they had passed notes to Stacy in 11th grade trigonometry class asking her to the homecoming dance and getting a "maybe" back and thinking that was pretty good. Others would be depressed because they hadn't gotten into the prelaw program at Cal, or would recall being excited by having bought their first car at twenty-two. None of the memories actually belonging to *them* in the way each of him would want to think they did.

They. They! Him. Each version of him suggested, written, modified, then tested by the dedicated computers Koss—one of them, anyway—had set up at various sites around the city and further out. Little Robbie factories, all trying to perfect Koss' dream of a code that could jump back and forth, of creating a *person* that didn't need to stay in one body. Program after program, Robbie after Robbie, written by computers toiling day and night at secured locations, each of them slightly different.

The ones that showed promise were downloaded into a body and sent out to try to achieve their goal, the reason for there being a Robbie—*Robbie**s***. The only unifying threads between them all were the underlying genetic code, stolen, as poetic justice, from the man who had killed Archie—and who, Robbie had learned along the way, had let this happen so he himself could become a code, be immortal if he wanted.

Well, that DNA and one other thing. All of them, every Robbie who got up out of a tank and went off into the world, would walk through their lives believing they loved Archie. Believing that because it had been written into their operating instructions. That line of code had stayed the same through the millions of permutations that had become *Robbie.* It was a part of him, as much a part of him as the instructions that made him grow ribs and eyes. Koss had made sure. He couldn't help loving Archie any more than he could help having legs.

*If you believed something was true was it true?*

In all, his entire mission took only minutes. Minutes were an eternity to him. It felt like several lifetimes he'd spent, living in this accelerated manner, whipping around as pure energy. But the speed served him because minutes were all he had to gather information, to send out instructions, to detail commands, and finally to leap one last time, running, running, running, jumping, flying, flying, flying.

*It was just like long jumping but nothing like it at all.*

It didn't matter how you fell in love, if you were in love. He loved her. No matter whether it came from that kiss in the dark or line 22,3224.5 of his code.

*Life is what you make of it.*
*I am, therefore I think.*
*I am, therefore I love.*

Landing. Landing. Landing.

**TRANSFER COMPLETE**

He opened the eyes of the body that waited for him in a small storage locker across town. He glanced around, carefully, as his eyes became able to focus. The tank automatically opened up and he was able to turn his head slightly, already. He saw two tanks, his own and another one sitting side by side.

They were powered by a portable generator which also kept running a handmade server that attached to a domain address registered, as the locker was, to a local drug dealer and general gadabout small time criminal who was available for hire by almost anyone, a guy named Charles but who almost everybody called Chip.

When he could sit up, he did, and staggered over to the small refrigerator that hummed quietly in the corner. He got out a protein drink and swallowed two-thirds of it almost in a single gulp, breathing heavily. The laptop on the table buzzed as a code he'd sent over to it finished copying and disconnected itself from the web. Robbie looked at the other tank, which held the dormant body of a grown woman with dirty blonde hair. *She's so beautiful*, Robbie thought.

He knew at least part of the reason he loved her was that she'd wanted him to always bring her back. But he hoped she'd written something into her own code about loving him back.

The screen of the laptop showed part of the message that had flashed over it. His message:

FIND ::embed:: OUT ::code:: WHO
::transfer:: YOU ::ht:cl:86.7:: ARE

Records show that over 157,000 codes have been created so far.

Codes are human.

Humans are codes.

Help them. Protect them.

And above all:

Use this fire wisely.

# ABOUT THE AUTHOR

In addition to writing this book, Briane Pagel has accomplished a lot of other things that somehow never managed to actually compensate, in his mom's eyes, for not becoming a doctor.

He achieved both a bachelor's and a law degree, and built not one but *three* successful practices. He raised, with the help of his wife, an entire family of five kids (or mostly, as the last two are only just 8 years old and still require a great deal of help, because *someone* has to be the bad guys when the action figures come out). Also, he invented the idea of "24 hours of pizza," which is brilliant even though society hasn't yet fully embraced the concept.

He lives in Middleton, Wisconsin, where he hasn't quit his day job. Yet.

www.ingramcontent.com/pod-product-compliance
Lightning Source LLC
Chambersburg PA
CBHW070950180726
48291CB00004B/1229